# THE FRENCH BREED

BY

## JAMES S. KELLY

ISBN: 978-1-963565-65-2 (Paperback)
ISBN: 978-1-963565-68-3 (Ebook)

Library of Congress Control Number: 2025901458

Printed in the United States of America

Published by:
info@thequippyquill.com
(302)-295-2278

# CONTENTS

# PROLOGUE

Max was born two years after his older brother Joe came into the world. The older son would grow up to be tall, rich and very powerful; Max would be energetic, charming and handsome. Their father accepted the second born and knew they'd have to find something for him to do. In this era, the oldest son would inherit the title. His mother Sophia was delighted with the precocious child. She knew that Max' father was the sire but she enjoyed the rumors that he was the love child of her liaison with a wealthy and important nobleman, who she knew and admired.

Her eldest son, Joe treated the second born with indifference and very little patience. He had little to do with young Max after he was ten years old, though the younger child followed him everywhere, trying to emulate Joe's expression, his walk and mannerisms. Max was mischievous and relished in teasing stoic Joe. The more Joe ignored Max, the more he would be a pain in the neck for his older sibling. To get Joe's attention, Max would hide the older boy's playthings. One of his favorite tricks was to throw Joe's covers out the third floor window on a cold night. He'd hide across the hall waiting for Joe to go to bed.

When Joe came running out of his room screaming obscenities at him, Max would run to his room and lock the door before Joe could get to him.

Max was never disciplined for these minor discretions, but that all came to a halt one day. Max was watching his brother and two of his friends play some form of dodge ball. Normally Joe would go into their house whenever he wanted to relieve himself if it was close by. Today, they were further away, so he went to one of the many stationary privies that frequented the estate and closed the door. Max was behind a tree watching him. Making sure Joe's playmates were distracted, Max dashed to the privy and put a wooden wedge in the crack. This held the door in place and prevented it from opening.

The two playmates drifted further away and couldn't hear Joe's cries for help. Max was still behind a tree about ten yards away but not too far that he didn't hear Joe scream that he was going to kill him when he got out of the privy. Max couldn't resist going by the door and telling Joe that he'd see him at supper.

It was one of the workers who heard Joe pleading for someone to open the door. When the workman opened the door, he was rebuked by Joe for taking his time. Joe went to the mansion and walked into his father's study and told him what happened.

"You know who locked me in." Josef screamed at his father..

"Max did, I presume."

"What are you going to about it?"

"A severe beating would be in order, but don't worry, I'll take care of it." He confined Max to his room for two days. It may have slowed him down a little, but he was back to his impish self within a week.

Joe was a natural victim for Max. As time went by, he made sure he wasn't in the same room with his younger brother. When his mother counseled Max on his behavior, he looked as though it was he who was the victim of such an accusation. "It wasn't me mama."

"I didn't say what you did." She countered.

"Well just in case, it wasn't me.

Since Joe was older, the privileges of the first born flowed to him and Max had to accept lesser rewards. This only widened the gap between the two. Max sought solace in his academics, becoming a brilliant student, but one who used his knowledge to berate his teachers and belittle his piers. He was especially astute in mathematics and he liked to bedevil his math teacher by asking him to solve nearly impossible equations. One day, Max asked his teacher to help with a particular problem. The unsuspecting lecturer put the equation on the blackboard and wrestled with it in front of the class. When the bell rang to change classes, the instructor was still working the puzzle which he never solved. Max and the other boys snickered behind his back.

The lecturer had the last laugh. He gave Max an average grade for the semester. Max was undaunted, he didn't slow his pace. Since scholastics was his forte, he raised the issue of his accomplishments to his parents any chance the four were together. He'd turn to Joe while the four were at the dinner table and ask him what he scored in Mathematics, Literature or another discipline, just to make Joe squirm. There were times when Joe was so mad that he'd leave the table and wouldn't return.

As they grew older, the separation widened and Max' biting humor didn't help; it was as though he couldn't control himself. Yet, he knew he'd made a mistake and when he was fifteen, he tried to rectify the situation but it was too late; Joe's wounds were too deep. Although Joe was the older and would inherit the family position, Max was the charmer and the ladies were enamored with Max' smile and good looks. Consequently, Max made a habit of seducing Joe's lady friends; in fact he made a habit of seducing his mother's friends.

Austria where the boys lived seemed to be at the heart of constant country to country uprisings and short little wars. Ferdinand, the boy's uncle, was the Emperor and a member of the Habsburg Family. The constant conflicts were too much for him to handle. He decided to resign in 1848 and named Joseph, who was only eighteen as his successor. The boy's father was stunned that his brother would ignore him and name his son as heir. Franz Joseph went on to reign for sixty eight years. Max had to content with being a lonely Archduke and his resentment grew; yet he masked it well. He was lively, charismatic and eager to please. He had to settle on being a welcome guest at dinner parties, dances and of course women.

# CHAPTER 1

The country to country flair ups continued after Franz Joseph was crowned Emperor. Unlike his uncle and the former Emperor, Franz decided to deal directly with the situations and with help from his brother Maximilian, he put down the little wars and peace came to the region. Max thought the animosity that Franz Josef felt for him was all but forgotten since Max helped him put down the armed revolts in the kingdom. But such was not the case.

Just out of his teenage years, he was looking for something to do, so he joined the small Austrian Navy.
This seemed to be Max' calling in life. As a Lieutenant, he made an unscheduled voyage through the Greek Islands and if that wasn't enough of an accomplishment, his brother appointed him Commander in Chief of the small Austrian Navy at the age of twenty-two.

The two men had diametrically opposed objectives with the appointment. Franz Josef knew he needed to give his brother a position in his administration. His mother and father were constantly reminding him that his brother was brilliant and it was an embarrassment to the family that the Emperor wouldn't help. Max couldn't believe the gift he received and he took to his new position like a salmon swimming upstream. He set out to modernize the Austrian Navy and initially he was very successful. But in so doing he took needed funds from training, supplies and other disciplines to modernize the fleet.

Franz Josef was furious. In essence he was a thrifty man and resented the lavish expenditures by his younger brother. Austria was a land locked nation and therefore didn't need a modernized Navy. The emperor's staff didn't help matters. They were continuously raising the issue of overspending by Max and asking the emperor what he was going to do about it.. Eventually, Franz Josef asked his mother to intercede with Max. When that didn't move Max, Franz Josef asked his father for help, but that didn't bear any fruit either. He felt that he had no alternative but to fire his brother.

But Max made a point. He showed that with proper leadership, the Austrian Navy could be an asset to the Austrian Army and its use should be included in any tactical strategy. Before he was dismissed, he travelled to the Iberian Peninsula and fell in love with both the

Portuguese and Adriatic Coasts. Max loved the sea and on one of his voyages, he purchased a plot of land on a hill overlooking the Adriatic Sea. He contracted for a beautiful estate called Miramare on the rocky promontory. However, completion of the dream estate took several years and Max never had time to spend it there for any length of time.

Prior to his dismissal, he met a young man at the Seville Fencing Academy of French heritage by the name of Robert St. Pierre. He was about the same age as Max, both were athletic and they instantly took a liking to each other. Once each week they'd meet at the academy; they used the same instructor. Both were good swordsmen but Max was slightly better. After a session of training at the academy, they'd share dinner together and got to know each other pretty well. They found that they had much in common especially when it came to women.

Needless to say many of the young women in the area admired the young men at the academy. Girls would wait outside the fencing academy on a Friday or Saturday Evening hoping to get an introduction to a rich young man. Over the next five years, even after Max was dismissed as head of the Austrian Navy, the two young men were inseparable. They could be seen evenings in

Vienna at one of elegant restaurants or in the front row of the symphony. There were always two young beautiful women with them and later there would be a party in Max' lodgings that would last all night.

One of the young women that Max was squiring around Vienna had been promised to another young man from a wealthy family. When the young man saw his intended at a table in the Café Bistro one evening, he took exception and challenged Max to a duel. The forbidden joust was scheduled at six the next morning behind the Austrian College of Arts. Robert St. Pierre was Max' second.

At the appointed time the two combatants met, as did the seconds and a magistrate to enforce the rules. Max opponent had more bravado than skill and the younger brother of the Emperor Franz Josef did everything he could not to kill the young man. When he pricked him in the shoulder, blood flowed and the contest concluded. Max apologized to the young man and promised to end his liaison with the man's intended. They shook hands and everything was settled as gentleman.

"You were lucky Max. What would you have done if he was as skilled as you?"

"I'd have to kill him."

"We should start making better choices in our women. You don't know what your brother would do if you killed a nobleman. He may have you hung." Both laughed and went to breakfast and then home for a nap, but the more Max thought about what his friend said, he wasn't sure what his brother would do in such a situation..

Max was the first of the two friends to get serious about a young woman. While at a ball in Vienna one evening, he met Viktoria Kesco and after a short romance the two fell in love. They were sure their parents and the Emperor would approve the union. They'd become intimate within the first two months of the romance and were very much in love. But a future between them wasn't to be. She was of a different religion and her father forbade the union. He took her home against her will and arranged a marriage to an older suitor. In spite of the disappointment, Max was to fall in love many times. On a cruise to Lisbon he met the beautiful Maria Amelia of Brazil. After a short courtship, they became engaged. However, the gods of love weren't smiling on Max.

Although his brother and Emperor approved of the union, Maria contracted Scarlet

Fever and wouldn't recover. She passed away shortly thereafter. Max was heart broken.

The good natured Max suffered two more devastating losses and sought solace in as many women as he could. He drank heavily and got into a few minor duels. Two opponents ended up with cut arms but a scandal, that a death would've caused, didn't happen. With him during this time was his pal, Robert St Pierre. He knew Max was morning and tried everything a friend could do to bring him back to reality. Robert acted as his confidant even though counseling Max at this time could be a waste of time. It would take another love affair to settle him down.

During the next few years, Max or as he was now called, Archduke Maximilian I, was being sent by his brother to various countries as an envoy or courier. Robert St. Pierre accompanied him as his aide. On a trip to France, where he was carrying a message from his brother to Napoleon III, he met the Emperor and his wife Eugenie. He found court life to be exciting and wondered if a crown was in his future. Napoleon found him to be a charming and invited him to spend a week at court.

One day at Versailles, he was introduced to a group of Mexican Conservatives who were trying to convince Napoleon that Mexico should be ruled by a monarchy, preferable from a European Nation. This was the first time that the Mexican's approached Max, dangling the position of Emperor of Mexico in front of him. Max was mildly flattered but really wasn't interested at this time; his head was still full of women, wine and having fun.

While Max was in Paris, Franz Joseph directed him ro go to Belgium before returning to Austria. He wanted Max to pay his respects to the newly crowned King Leopold of Belgium. That's when he met Charlotte, the daughter of King Leopold. A romance blossomed between the two and the Court of Belgium was anticipating a scandal. The young couple made no secret of their affair. They were spending most of their time at a country home of her parents, unchaperoned. So enamored with Max was Charlotte, that the petite Princess was the aggressor.

King Leopold sent for Max and suggested that Max propose to Charlotte. Max was ready and wondered why he didn't think of that. That afternoon he made his future father-in-law and bride very happy. The couple married in Brussels the following month, after Franz Joseph approved of the Union and even attended the ceremony, along with his mother and father. The marriage also solidified the role of Belgium as a friendly power to the Habsburg Family. Soon thereafter Maximilian I was appointed Viceroy of Lombardy- Venetia. He and Charlotte moved to Milan, as did Robert St Pierre and his new bride, Sophia.

.Sophia was the daughter of an Army General in the Belgian Armed Forces. She was a friend of Charlotte and it was the young princess who introduced her to Robert. The couple was married a month after Max and Charlotte's ceremony. King Leopold offered him a commission in the Belgian Army. But Max and Robert had been friends too long to make a change. When Max said he'd like Robert to be his aide permanently, he accepted immediately.

After a brief visit to Milan, Max and Charlotte continued their honeymoon wit a cruise to the Adriatic and lived at Max' Miramare Estate for a short period of time. They invited Robert and Sophia to join them after their  own honeymoon. Robert St. Pierre and his bride Sophia arrived a month later and the two couples stayed another two months.

As with the Austrian Navy when he was the commander, Max set about with zeal to properly administer his new position. He installed many liberal reforms without Franz Josef's permission or at least a concurrence from the emperor's staff. Robert tried to get him to slow down his zeal, but Max was undaunted. Again, he alienated the people he needed to help implement his policies. It was a constant battle with his brother who wouldn't give any concessions to the people. Robert tried to act as mediator with the Emperor's staff with only moderate success.

Although Max' policies seemed practical, Franz Joseph's staff felt otherwise. They were constantly interfering and delaying correspondence between Max and his brother. Since they had the Emperor's ear, it was inevitable what would happen. Max may have been ahead of his time, but he was out of a job. Here was a person who knew how to think outside the envelope, but it wasn't to be. The time he lived in didn't favor liberal leanings. This commitment to liberal ideas would eventually be the undoing of Maximilian. His main fault was that he wasn't realistic.

Having led the Austrian Navy and been replaced by his brother and then appointed as Viceroy and replaced by his brother, Max was bitter and sought the arms of other women to sooth his bruised ego. He knew he had the people in mind when he made changes to the strict conservative views of the Habsburg Dynasty. He just didn't understand the term, go slowly, when making major changes. His brother felt threatened by any concession and therefore wouldn't support him. He should have given Franz Josef a plan and at least received some sort of an agreement before he instituted sweeping reforms.

The Conservative Group in Mexico persisted and sent Jose Hidalgo to France to see if he could stir up some interest with the Europeans to support a Mexican Monarchy. Hidalgo was sponsored by the Santa Anna Government. However, Santa Anna was replaced and Hidalgo had no status in Europe. Still the concept didn't go away and Max was approached again by some Mexican Conservatives to see if he was interested.

"Where is the support coming from for a monarchy?" Max asked the emissary.

"There are several factions that favor a monarchy. The first is the Catholic Church. Most Mexicans are catholic and therefore take direction from their parish priests. The second group is the noblemen, who are conservative by nature and like the stability of the monarchy and third is the Mexican Population. The constant changeover of governments always leaves them in a vacuum. They need stability."

"I can understand the desire of the Catholic Church and the Mexican noblemen to lean toward a monarchy, but I still have problem with the general population. Why should I believe that they would welcome a foreign monarch?"

"The life of the villagers centers on the church. The priest is the go-between. He performs marriages. baptizes children, conducts services every Sunday, hears the confessions of everyone and provides guidance during their lifetime. He's with them from birth until death."

St. Pierre was more candid than any of Max' advisors and felt his friend needed to have his eyes opened. "This is a third world country and you don't speak the language. You have no feel for what the people want. Who will support you when the going gets rough. The priest is the most important man in the village, but he owes his allegiance to his church. You could come into conflict with him and where would that leave you??"

"Napoleon has assured me that he will stay the course or at least until we can successfully establish the monarchy. I believe him."

"Do you really think that Napoleon can be trusted? He's a politician and is looking out for number one. How long do you think I'll take to institute the reforms you have in mind. These people are most illiterate and are used to taking direction. Even so, Juarez and Diaz were only in power a short time. The conservatives have ruled before those two and many of their laws are still in place. They'll see you as a short time reformer."

"France has a huge stake in the outcome. They provided substantial funding to the Juarez Government and haven't received any interest let alone principal payments. Yes I think he can be trusted because he wants France's investment repaid."

"In addition, I was told by the conservatives from Mexico that I can rely on them and their friends."

"The Mexican elite will look out for themselves and make any deal to protect what they have. They lost to the liberals and are looking to return to power, so they'll say anything. What have they got to lose? They're out of power now and only a European supported Monarchy gives them a chance to return to power at no cost to them. They don't know you; you're just an instrument to help them gain access to power."

"Napoleon's wife has encouraged me and the Mexican Conservatives feel the people in Mexico will respond to a monarchy. I'm convinced that I'll succeed."

"Sure they did. You're a member of the Habsburg Family and your brother, the Emperor, is a valuable ally. But this is Napoleon's game and you aren't privy to what's in his mind. Let's be realistic. The Mexican Conservatives were defeated by the liberals and they want to be back in power again. They'll say anything to get someone like Napoleon interested."

"I talked to several bishops and they feel the power of the Catholic Church will keep the peasants in line."

"The church will support you as long as you adhere to their views. Remember they supported the conservatives in Mexico. What does that tell you, You're hanging everything on Napoleon's word and that the Mexican people will support your reforms. They've never been in power. They're used to obeying the law whoever issues it. They are not a group you can rely on."

"I'll have them sweeten the deal if they want me to go over there and not be just a figurehead."

From Charlotte's perspective, Max possessed credentials that were hard to ignore by those who wanted a monarchy established in Mexico.. He was a member of the Habsburg Family and had proved to be a more than an adequate administer as Viceroy in Lombardy and Commander of the Austrian Navy. In addition, he had Napoleon's ear and French troops to rely upon. Besides, Charlotte wanted to be Empress and Max wanted an empire. He looked around and assessed what was available to him. There really wasn't a position that suited him or that his brother would let him fill. He could only serve in whatever capacity his brother wanted at the moment. There was no choice; he had to go to Mexico. Franz Josef had two sides and one of his sides remembered his childhood and all the animosity he had for Max, so he wasn't going to give him some plum position.

Fate sometimes enters a situation and decides the outcome. Benito Juarez was the President of Mexico and suspended payments on all foreign debt incurred by the Mexican Conservatives when they were in power. All that did was provide an opening for Napoleon III, who had aspirations not only on Mexico but America as well. The sale of Louisiana still left a sour taste on the French palate

Though Lincoln counseled Napoleon against any French ambitions in the Americas, the Union's hands were tied. They were deeply involved in a civil war with the revolting Southern States. The French sought support from Spain and England who also had invested with the conservatives in Mexico and therefore weren't getting paid.. Their plan was. to renegotiate the Mexican debt with Juarez.

The three nations conducted a conference to establish the negotiating ground rules. However, it became apparent that France didn't want to renegotiate repayment of the debt. They wanted to invade Mexico, oust the Juarez Government and take over part of the country. England and Spain saw the handwriting on the wall and dropped out of the negotiations,

The French invaded Mexico in 1862 joined by many of the Mexican Conservative Generals, but the expeditionary force was too small and the planning inadequate. They landed in

Vera Cruz and started moving toward the capitol in Mexico City. They suffered an astonishing defeat by an undermanned Mexican Army under Benito Juarez at the Battle of Puebla on May 5, 1862. This victory was commemorated in the future as Cinco de Maio.

The humiliating defeat angered Napoleon III. He sent almost 39,000 more troops to Mexico, but it still took them a year to capture Puebla and later Mexico City. There was no doubt in Max's mind that he wanted to be Emperor of Mexico. He established two conditions for his acceptance. He wanted the support of France and England and he insisted on a mandate from the majority of the Mexican people.

England decided not to get involved. So that condition couldn't be met. The French controlled a portion of Mexico, where most of the Mexican population lived. They told Max that since they controlled most of the population in Mexico that should suffice for the second condition. Max couldn't control his enthusiasm to be named Emperor, so he agreed that the second condition had been met. But Franz Joseph hadn't been heard from.

He notified Max that he wouldn't release him unless Max signed away any claim he had to the Austrian Throne. Max demanded an audience with Franz Joseph to argue against relinquishing his right to succession. The two met in Franz Joseph's private office. "Why should I want to give up my rights and why should you demand it?"

"To become Emperor of Mexico, you naturally give up your rights as a citizen of Austria and therefore become a citizen of a foreign nation. Not only that, but if you agree to go, I'll strip you of your title as Archduke of Austria.

"But Napoleon III and his wife are standing behind me. It's as though I'm working for them, not the Mexicans."

"Even more so, If you're but a tool of France, then I don't want to attach my government to that endeavor."

"Are you sure this isn't just a petty ploy on your part to get back at me for the things between us as kids?"

"We'll never know will we?"

Max was furious but there was nothing he could do. St. Pierre was waiting for him outside Franz Joseph's office. When Max told him what was discussed, St Pierre responded. "There's no backup position if going to Mexico doesn't work out. I don't trust that Napoleon will back you all the way. Losing your succession rights is too much to give up, Franz Joseph could die tomorrow and you'd be left out of everything. It's not worth it Max. You should stay here as Archduke and take your chances. At least talk it over with Charlotte. She has a keen sense of the politics involved."

Charlotte felt the opportunity in Mexico was enormous and recommended that Max agree to take the position. Two years after the first French Troops met defeat outside Vera Cruz, Maximilian I and his wife Charlotte arrived in Vera Cruz. They were accompanied by Robert St. Pierre and his wife, Sophia.

# CHAPTER 2

Reluctantly, Max agreed to give up his succession to the throne in Austria. He fought hard to retain his title of Archduke but finally had to give that up as well. Franz Josef wouldn't agree to release him to go to Mexico until he did. With that final concession, Max was able to accept Napoleon offer to be Emperor of Mexico.

Napoleon was pleased and sent his country's best ocean liner to pick up Max and Charlotte in Trieste. The couple wanted to visit Miramare on the peninsula before they left for the greatest adventure of their lives. They hadn't visited the estate for over a year and the month they spent here before boarding the French Liner, Escadrille was the happiest month of their marriage.

Robert and Sophia joined them the last two weeks of their stay. Sophia had given birth to two boys, two years apart. Though they were married for nearly the same number of years, Charlotte and Maximilian were childless.

As they boarded the liner, a band played the Austrian national anthem. Their stateroom had been upgraded and the voyage to the new world was wonderful. Max and Charlotte had one stop to make on the way to Mexico.. He felt it necessary to secure the blessing of the Pope. The Italian King greeted them as a head of state when they arrived at a port thirty miles from Rome. They travelled by carriage with an entourage of soldiers escorting them to the Italian palace.

The audience with the pope was scheduled for the following day. For whatever reason, the Vatican postponed it for a week. Max and Charlotte made the most of their time in the eternal city by attending the opera and being the guests of honor at two balls given by the Italian nobility. When the audience with the pope took place, Max was lectured for an hour by his holy father on the rights the church had in Mexico. He made Max promise that he would always look out for the church while he was Emperor.

Max had been encouraged by some European Monarchs while he was in Rome, but there were many who felt that he didn't have a chance to bring stability to a country in chaos. Newly promoted by the future Emperor, Colonel Robert St. Pierre, his wife Sophia and their two young boys accompanied the future Emperor on their cruise to Mexico. Each was in the early stages of their marriage and enjoyed the voyage to the new world. They were in essence, the only passengers on board the liner. They played cards, shuffle board and enjoyed luxurious meals every evening

When they were insight of Vera Cruz, everyone became excited. The women dressed in their finest. Charlotte put on her favorite jewels and was ready to meet the crowds gathered at the port. When they arrived in Vera Cruz in 1964 and got off at the pier, they were disappointed that there was only a sparse crowd to greet them. Max was led to believe that the entire country was behind his monarchy. Vera Cruz was a primitive seaside town and not what Max expected. Charlotte was especially disappointed and voiced her concern to Max.

"Napoleon assured us that we would be welcomed with opened arms. If that's true, then where is everyone?"

"The majority of the peasant population is centered in the Mexico City vicinity. I have no choice but to assume that we will be greeted by many more people when we get there."

They soon made their way to Mexico City where their reception was more in line with what a visiting monarch would receive. Most of the noblemen and their wives and the Bishop of

Mexico City were in attendance along with the French General, Marcel Petard. .Max was crowned Maximilian I shortly thereafter and a smile spread across his face and that of Charlotte's when the bishop placed the crown on Max' head.

Initially, they took up residence at the National Palace in Mexico City, but they subsequently moved to Chapultepec Castle located on a hill in the outskirts of Mexico City. Robert, Sophia and Family were given quarters near the palace.

Prior to the Emperor's occupancy, he had the castle refurbished and a boulevard constructed that led directly to Mexico City. He patterned the road after the grand boulevards in Europe and. named the promenade after his wife Charlotte. The history of the castle went back as far as the Aztecs and more recently the Spanish Viceroys.

Max wasn't entirely naïve about his new position. He knew he had to rely on the support of the French Army to survive in this third world country. To facilitate the perception of the power transfer from President Juarez to himself, he needed the friendship of the Mexican Conservative Generals. But their support and help paled in comparison to the help the French

Army could provide if they wanted to. It didn't take long for Max and his inner circle to understand that the French Generals looked upon Maximilian as nothing more than a pawn of Napoleon. He had to gain the support of the Mexican people or he and his Empress would be holed up in some Castle entirely at the mercy of the French.

The second political reality that Maximilian had to face was that although the Mexican Conservatives petitioned France to have the Monarchy, Napoleon III wanted Max to have liberals in his cabinet and to institute some liberal policies as soon as possible. On the other side, the Conservatives in the cabinet wanted Max to reverse the liberal policies instituted by President Juarez. So Max had to walk a tight rope between the conservatives and liberals. Napoleon didn't give Max any advice on how to accomplish that feat.

Not only that, but Napoleon was working behind the scenes in the new Empire.. He instituted a policy known only to his French Commanders in Mexico, to marginalize the conservatives whenever possible. The reality of the situation was that Max was nothing but a figurehead. Napoleon III was pulling the strings. He was directing and financially supporting the French Army in Mexico.

Max saw the situation that was unfolding and he didn't like it. With Robert's help, Max tried to reform the Imperial Mexican Army and put it under Maximilian's control. Under orders from Napoleon III, General Bazaine, the French Commander, interceded and Max was denied that military support that would have given him some leverage with Napoleon. "Max you need to send an emissary to Napoleon and see if he'll concede an army loyal to you. If not, we have no place here. I'd advise you to give him a thirty-day ultimatum. Either let you have an army or you abdicate." Robert St. Pierre advised.

"I can't do that. I must figure out how to make it work with what I have. If I abdicate, where would I go? My brother has basically taken away my citizenship and Napoleon III would never forgive me if I abdicate."

"I know it's a bold initiative, but if Napoleon thinks you'll cave into any order he issues, you'll never be able to rule. What have you got to lose? The French Army ignores you and Napoleon won't give you the resources you need to rule."

Robert was an astute political student. He knew that Napoleon's real objective was to gain a foothold in the Americas. Max was the vehicle that he was using to gain that position. Napoleon wasn't about to pull out in the near future if he could increase his influence. Robert was vocal about his position. He wanted Max to take a hard-line position with Napoleon. "Now's the time to send an emissary to France and clearly state your position. You are in a very strong position now. Perhaps later, you won't be able to have a voice." Robert spoke but he wasn't sure Max was listening.

Maximilian's initial decree was in the form of amnesty for the liberals. He ran this policy by his cabinet but they were at an impasse. The liberals hated the conservatives and vice versa. Max even went as far as to offer amnesty to Juarez and the post of Prime Minister in his government. But Juarez declined. In a written response, Juarez firmly stated that he was the elected President of Mexico and he was going to fight to recover his country. Robert told Max that the decree wouldn't bear any fruit, but the Emperor said he had to take a chance and see if he could get Juarez to listen and do what was best for the country.

Juarez had vacated the capitol of Mexico because of the overwhelming strength of the French. However, he established a government in the northern part of the country and made that it a no-go zone for the French. The French Commander in that region tried to break through the Mexican lines, but they were beaten back on three occasions.

To make matters worse, Juarez appointed Matais Romero as ambassador to The United States. Romero was articulate and a man who could ably communicate Juarez' claim as the sole ruler of Mexico. The result was that the US wouldn't recognize the ambassador that Maximilian sent to Washington nor would the US sent a representative to Mexico.

The influence of the Catholic Church in Mexico was enormous. Juarez sought to limit their privileges and power. The methods he used were significant and the church leaders in Mexico and the Vatican were furious. Initially, he tried confiscation of their property through forced sales. Next, he instituted freedom of religion, removing Catholicism as the sole religion of the country. The nation was predominately catholic and the citizens of the small towns in the country all looked to the local priest for guidance. What Juarez ordered wasn't popular and the people wouldn't comply, but it still was a thorn in the side of the church.

Sometime after Maximilian took power, he was visited by the papal nuncio who directed that the liberal laws put in place by Juarez should be outlawed. Specifically, the nuncio directed that all property confiscated from the church by the Juarez Regime would be returned to each diocese. In addition, religious tolerance would be rescinded and Catholicism would be the only religion authorized in Mexico.

Max was inclined to agree, but he wanted to run it by Napoleon III. When the word came back that Napoleon refused the nuncio's demands, Max was shocked. The papal nuncio wrote a very strong letter threatening loss of support to Maximilian. This was a major blow to his government and for the liberal agenda he had in mind. He wrote another letter to Napoleon asking if the Emperor made a mistake in refusing the Nuncio's requests. The answer came via the Commanding French General in Mexico. He was terse when he said, "the Emperor says he didn't get it wrong."

The two friends went riding north of Mexico City. Six of the bodyguards who were assigned to the Emperor made the trip with St. Pierre and Max. They stopped along a stream to cool off while the six bodyguards kept lookout. Max told Robert what the papal nuncio threatened, what Napoleon said in his first letter and then repeated via his Commander.

"Max, you're in a no win situation. You may think you're the Emperor, but Napoleon controls the French Army and their commander won't permit you to have an army loyal to you. With the church threatening you, who will support you, certainly not the peasants? The people in all the towns owe their allegiance to the parish priest. What do you think his position will be? His loyalty is to his bishop and ultimately to the pope. The only support you have in this country is the conservatives. If you limit their influence, they'll withdraw from you and where does that leave you?"

"I know. I know. I agree with everything you say. My only salvation is the reforms I can make for the Mexican people. I need their friendship and if I have it, the French will support me."

"The French don't listen to the people. They look upon them as a conquered people. We have to be careful, my friend. None of your inner circle speaks Spanish. I've met a young Captain by the name of Jose Santana. He could be an asset to you. His family is well known in Mexico City and he has a keen sense of what's going on.

At present, he's an aide to General Quintero. I know the general quite well. I can ask him to permit Santana to function as your aide."

"I think we can't have enough friends. Set up an appointment. I'd like to interview him."

Jose Santana was a welcome surprise to Max. His resume reflected that he grew up in Mexico City in an affluent family. His father was a well known attorney in the capitol and his uncle, a wealthy land owner had been an advisor to the conservative Prime Minister. His uncle's children were physicians and educators. Jose spent a year in France studying Political Science and then returned to Mexico with a commission in the conservative army under General Quintero. The young Mexican was fluent in both Spanish and French and was married to his childhood sweetheart, Angelica. The couple had no children.

In his interview with Max at the palace, he was quick on his feet and had no problem answering all of Max' questions. He was hired on the spot and Robert, as Chief of Staff, made an arrangement with General Quintero to release the young Mexican and transfer him to Max' staff.. From this point forward, Max, Robert and Jose Santana would spend a lot of time together enjoying sparring with sabers.

Robert filled in the parts not found in the resume. "He's handy with a sword and pistol and plays polo at his
father's club. He's fought two duels; neither of his opponents died. He's fearless in a crisis and knows most of the conservative generals in Mexico.

Max was always looking for ways to ingratiate himself with the common people of Mexico. He and Charlotte talked about it and finally she agreed with Max that if it would help, she would do it. The Empress agreed to change her name from Charlotte to Carlotta in order to impress the Mexican people. Initially, there was much to do about the name change, but as time went on, it was only a footnote in the history books.

She and Max didn't have any children. The rumor was that Max had contacted Syphilis from his numerous mistresses and passed it on to Carlotta. The Emperor hadn't changed his bachelor ways and had many liaisons. In spite of his infidelities, Carlotta was enamored with and devoted to the handsome Austrian. On one occasion, she came face to face with Lady Angelina, the most recent Maximilian conquest. Although it was embarrassing for the two women, Carlotta politely acknowledged the woman and then went on her way. She didn't mention the incident to her husband.

Carlotta was quite politically astute. So when Max would make state visits to visit the Governors in other parts of the country, it was Carlotta who stayed at the castle and functioned as regent. She'd greet emissaries from other countries, discuss trade and would host some of the guests for a week at a time. It was not uncommon for her to sign country to country agreements. There were rumors, as is the case in most governments that one or two of the male guests visited her in her chambers after dark. She refuted the rumors and Max made no mention of them.

True to his word and being a liberal at heart, Max worked long hours trying to see which laws needed to be changed, which were obsolete and which needed to be extended. The enormity of the volumes of laws issued by Maximilian during his time as Emperor, in spite of the opposition from the conservatives in his cabinet and the conservative critics outside the government, was overwhelming.

His critics lashed back at him stating that all the laws he issued had been enacted before by the Juarez Government. But Max was undaunted. He knew he was right to go to all this effort; he was the champion of the people. To show that he was more than someone who pushed for more laws and was actually a statesman, he openly courted immigration from the United States and two communities of Americans were established in Mexico. Both communities flourished even after Max was no longer Emperor. He didn't want to sit on his throne and have his staff tell him what was going on in the country. He went to all the communities surrounding Mexico City on an annual basis and pitched his policies. He was bent on bringing the Mexican People to his side. H spent much of his time with the parish priests in the towns he visited and always gave money to the charity of the priest's choice.

# CHAPTER 3

Max wasn't dumb; he may have been naïve in taking the position of Emperor of Mexico, but he had values and wanted to make life for the average Mexican much better. Some of his initiatives that were put on the books such as a law giving a living wage to the Mexican Peasants, free schools for all, outlawing corporal punishment and limiting inheritance of debt were farsighted. He just didn't sit back and issue laws or decrees, he visited many towns in the nation to sell his ideas and see how the laws that were enacted were being implemented.

But the result of all his laws was that, the French tolerated them, the conservatives fought them tooth and nail, the liberals sat back waiting for the Juarez Government to return and the peasants didn't comprehend them.

The civil war in The United States ended and although the US didn't send troops to Mexico to support Juarez, they gave him a thirty million dollar loan and refused to recognize the Maximilian Government. Additionally, some Americans joined the Juarez army to fight the French. There were many disillusioned

Confederate Soldiers, who couldn't go back home because there was nothing left. They went to Mexico because they were hiring. Consequently, the French deployed many of their troops in the northern part of the country which led to a surge in guerrilla warfare in the south. But this deployment of French Troops to the north wasn't Maximilian's idea. He wasn't consulted. Robert St. Pierre said it best, "How can you run a country when the men you need to keep you in power are controlled by someone else?"

Max still had some conservative support but it was slowly moving out of the capitol. At one point he didn't have an escort to visit a neighboring community because the French General controlling that area wouldn't send anyone to assist him, There was an increase in guerrilla warfare around Mexico City, Roving bands of ten or more were looting small businesses and make the populace nervous. Max was confined to his quarters many times because he didn't have an escort that would ensure his safety, when traveling the short distance to the capitol..

Max had about two dozen armed guards at his disposal but these weren't the kind of men that had any loyalty to the Emperor. Using them as an escort was too great a risk and he needed more men under his control. He needed men he could trust.

The French Army was constantly under attack. Juarez didn't confront the French head on; he'd wait until they were in the countryside attending to some function before his men would attack. It was mostly hit and run tactics but the toll was the same. They'd attack, kill two or three French soldiers and then make their way out of harm's way.

To counterbalance these attacks, The French Army Commander demanded that Max institute a decree that would punish anyone interfering with the French. Robert and Jose Santana argued against the decree but Max felt he was forced to issue the Black Decree. There was a moment when he realized that the decree was toxic and tabled it's release. The French Army Commander visited the palace and demanded that M<ax issue the order. In actuality, he threatened to pull all support for the Emperor if the Black Decree wasn't issued in three days.

It was a complicated law that attorneys could argue in court over, It firmly stated that anyone collaborating with the guerrillas would be executed. The problem with the new law was that there wasn't an independent assessment for anyone being charged. If the French Soldiers arrested someone who violated this law, he was automatically found guilty. Too often, bystanders, who didn't help the French were found to be complicit and arrested. If Max wanted to win over the nation, he should have resisted the French in issuing the decree. Over eleven thousand Mexicans were executed as a result of this decree and Maximilian's popularity sunk to its lowest level. Those around Maximilian I saw that the end was in sight.

While the American Civil War was raging, Napoleon felt embolden to remain in Mexico. This third world country was but a stepping stone to his ultimate goal. He wanted California. However as soon as the Civil W ended, the Juarez' government was recognized by the American President and a loan made, Napoleon knew the handwriting was on the wall and he could not succeed against the battle tested American nation. In January 1966, Napoleon told his cabinet that he intended to remove all French Troops from Mexico. Max sent a courier to France to plead with Napoleon to grant him a little more time until some of his liberal initiatives would bear fruit, but Napoleon responded negatively; he said it was too expensive an enterprise and that Maximilian hadn't won over the Mexican People. In a leisurely moment with

Robert, Max said. "You were right Robert. Napoleon will not support me. I'm on my own. It might have been different if the southern states had made good on their revolt, but with the north in charge, it isn't worth it to Napoleon to honor his pledge to me."

When Max told Carlotta what Napoleon intended, she cried. "He and Eugenie promised they would see this through. Did you have an argument with him?"

"No. I pleaded with him to stay another year and let some of the liberal laws take effect, but he said no."

"Where does this leave us?" Carlotta asked.

"I can't go home. Franz Josef has stripped me of my citizenship and I'm a man without a country."

"Father could find a position for you in the Belgium Government. He always liked you. Your father and mother love you. They would help."

"Franz stripped me of my title as Archduke as well. There's nothing left for me at home. This has to work if I'm to have anything in this lifetime."

"There must be someone we can reach out to that will help. What if I go to Europe and appeal to Eugenie?"

"Napoleon is difficult to approach. Perhaps you're right. Eugenie may be the only one that can salvage this situation. It'll take a month to get ready and I want to talk with you about the trip.

One month later Carlotta and her entourage made the trip to Vera Cruz accompanied by fifty troops assigned the French General, by loaned to Max for this one trip. They were commanded on the trip be Colonel St. Pierre and his aide Captain Santana. Carlotta took most of her clothes and jewelry and some personal items. What surprised Robert St. Pierre was that her personal items filled up eight large wagons.

The parting of Maximilian and Carlotta was emotional. Carlotta cried and kissed him with all the passion she could muster. "I'll be back in four months Max. I won't desert you. You are my love."

The Empress of Mexico arrived in France, made her way to Paris and immediately sought an audience with Napoleon and Eugenie. It took a week, but she persevered; Eugenie said she was sorry, but Napoleon said he wasn't going to spend anymore money on the venture,

"But sir, you promised to support Maximilian until his position was stable."

"Madam, I've a country to run and the cost to keep your husband in power is impacting my country. I bid you good day."

Undaunted,, Carlotta .met with several heads of European Countries including her father., but she was unable to gain any support for Max. The most important audience never took place. Franz Josef refused to meet with her. She pushed herself to try to salvage something for Max, but all she got in return was that her mental health was deteriorating and she remained in Europe under the care of physicians. She divided her time between Miramare on the Adriatic Coast and her family in Belgium.. She never saw Maximilian again, though they corresponded until he was executed.

After the order was given by Napoleon III to withdraw the French Army in Mexico, Robert

St. Pierre and Captain Jose Santana begged Max to leave with the French. "I've worked so hard for the people of Mexico. I believe they'll support me."

"Max, this is folly. The Black Decree fired up the haters within the masses. Many of the towns where people were killed because of your edict, have hung you in effigy. Without the French, we don't have a chance. The French have suggested you leave with them. Let's do it."

"It's too late. I've already communicated my intent to stay here and fight on. I'll appeal to the nation. I've proposed a cease fire to Juarez, so that a national election can be held to see who the people want to lead them. I plan to see it through. There are many in Mexico counting on me to bring stability to this country. I can't let them down. Besides, where would I go? This is it. My brother has stripped me of my title and my country. I have to make this work."

When St. Pierre brought the devastating news to Max that Juarez refused a ceasefire, and there would be no national election, Max was undaunted. He felt that with his Army of Conservatives, numbering around ten thousand men, he could fight on.

"Max, we must leave the country while we have a chance. Soon Juarez will cut off all our escape routes. He has too many men on his side. What good is it if he captures us? He'll put us all before a firing squad. His army chants a slogan to hang you before Christmas."

At home, Robert's wife voiced her concern. "With the French leaving, how can we survive? They hate us here. Doesn't Max see that?"

"Max is an isolated ruler. He sees what he wants to see. He feels that the laws he enacted help the peasants. He can't see that the church is against him and therefore the parish priests are not supporting him. And who do the people listen to?"

"The parish priest. Is there any hope for our family?"

"I can't get him to listen to me. I've given him an escape plan, but he says for me, Santana and our families to leave; he's staying."

"We're not going to stay are we?"

"No. We're leaving soon. There's a few issues I need to resolve first."

As the last French Troops were leaving the country, Max was starting to realize how feeble his position was. He assembled what was left of his supporters and marched to the city of Queretaro. They had to march by protesters as they entered the city, shouting kill the Emperor. The liberal generals under Juarez immediately laid siege to the city with forty thousand troops. St. Pierre and Santana presented another escape plan to Max but he refused. "I know you have my best interests at heart, but I can't leave while there's still a chance. I suggest you use the plan and take your families out of here."

"We can't leave without you." St. Pierre said.

"Nonsense. I order you and Santana to escape. I'll be fine."

The siege was suffocating the inhabitants of the city. St. Pierre went to Max again and asked him to leave with them. The water supply to the city had been cut off by Juarez and food was scarce. There were riots in the streets that were put down by Max supporters. Yet, many of his soldiers were deserting and going over to Juarez . Max spent most of his time sitting in his office. He was becoming a recluse.

Jose's father was able to send ten thousand Pesos with a short note to his son, so they had at least some money to live on. The note said that their position was hopeless and for Jose to think of his family and let Max hang if that's what he wanted. One of the exit gates out of the city was less guarded and St. Pierre bribed the Lieutenant in charge to look the other way. "Robert, you and Santana must leave. They won't harm me." Max said

The two men and their families and four bodyguards went through the west gate of the city around midnight and made their way north. They were dressed as peasants and their mode of transportation was four burros and two wagons with some of the family furniture. They were traveling heavy. Knowing that they were going to travel a long distance, Jose and Robert reinforced the two wagons.

They left Queretaro shortly after midnight in the direction of San Luis Potosi and tried their best to stay off the main road. They were able to skirt two check points but on the third day they were intercepted by six of Juarez' soldiers and had to shoot their way clear. Two of their bodyguards were killed and all six of the Juarez troops were killed. They continued north without burying their friends. The children were unharmed but the two wives were shaken up and Sophia voiced her concern. "Did you have to kill all six? They'll hunt us down like dogs and hang us all."

"There was no choice. If we left them alive they would have gone for help and perhaps we would've suffered the same fate." Robert responded.

One thing Santana and St. Pierre were knowledgeable about was the strength and location of the Mexican Army in the northern part of the country. In order to reach the United States they would have to navigate around their outposts. Juarez had set up check points all over the northern part of Mexico to capture any fleeing conservatives, Santana, with his grasp of the Spanish Language, had successfully gotten them through two of those check points. Their next main town they'd have to get by was Tamvalipas.

"As we get closer to the border, they're going to check us more thoroughly as we pass." Jose told Robert.

"I know."

When they were near Ciudad Vittoria, they stopped at a check point that four Mexican Soldiers were guarding. Santana presented everyone's forged passes to the Corporal in charge.. Initially, he waved them through, but one of the soldiers asked Robert in Spanish, where they were going. Robert's Spanish was limited and though he tried to explain where they were headed, the soldier was suspicious and the other three soldiers sensed something was wrong and started to raise their weapons

Robert drew his handgun and killed the soldier who became suspicious. Jose shot another and the two bodyguards handled the others including the Corporal. "I'm sorry, but I couldn't take a chance. We need to bury them quickly and get out of here." Robert told the others.

They buried the dead men and continued northeast toward the American border. They knew that the Juaristas would be coming after them and they had to hurry. The next day, as they hid behind some brush, there were six riders in uniform who rode east of them. They waited thirty minutes before they continued on. The children were now a liability, because they could cry at any minute. They had to travel at night if possible. Sophia was upset. "Why did we have to kill the soldiers back there? They were only doing their jobs. Is this is how it's going to be at every check point?"

"I'm sorry Sophia but I felt that they needed to be eliminated if we were to escape. If we tied them up and they freed themselves, we'd be in jeopardy. I couldn't take a chance that they'd get help and hunt us down. Our children's lives are more important to me than the soldiers I killed." This seemed to appease his wife. Robert wondered what would happen if they met other soldiers?

They traveled mostly at night and hid out during the daytime while they were sleeping. This presented several problems. One was the wagons could easily get bogged down because they couldn't see the terrain very clearly. One night they were travelling off the main road and got stuck in some fine sand. It took them the entire night to free the wheels even though they unloaded most of what the wagon was carrying.

Ten days later, they reached the outskirts of Matamoros; everyone was exhausted. Santana found a fisherman who had a small flat bottom barge type boat that could carry them across to Brownsville Texas. Sensing that the group was fleeing Mexico, the fisherman demanded an exorbitant amount to take them across. Rather than resort to violence, Jose negotiated firmly and although he paid more than he wanted, he did it without any bloodshed.

They chose a night when it was raining and entered the Gulf of Mexico three miles south of Matamoros.  Luckily, they didn't meet any other boats and landed on the beach east of Brownsville. The only problem they encountered was the weight of the furniture. They had to make two trips. The boatman wanted more money, but Jose said no. He made sure that he traveled back and forth with the owner of the boat. When he finally offloaded at Matamoros, he paid the balance agreed on plus a bonus, and everyone was happy.

"If there's anyone that comes asking for us, I'll assume it was you that told them. I'll find you and that boat of yours will be no more." The eyes of the boat owner said it all.

The two Mexican bodyguards fell on the beach and kissed the sand. Though they escaped from a dangerous situation, the six adults knew they still had to be aware that Juarez may have spies in the states. They spent a week in a small town east of Brownsville, resting, tending to Robert's and Sophia's two children, buying supplies and repairing the two wagons.

They learned from the Mexicans living in the town that Maximilian had been captured. One of the merchants told Jose that Mexican soldiers were looking for a group that murdered six soldiers at a check point in the north central part of Mexico and killed and buried four at another checkpoint near Ciudad Vittoria. Though the Mexicans were checking south of the border, the American Border Patrol was given Robert and Jose's description. Robert decided they'd better move on.

# CHAPTER 4

The Spanish papers in the United States covered the trial of Maximilian. The newspapers left an impression that the former Emperor would be found guilty and the European powers would then intercede on his behalf and he'd be allowed to leave the country. Juarez felt threatened by the Emperor's presence and didn't want him to remain in the country. He also wanted to send a message to anyone who thought about invading his country.

A reward was offered by the Mexican Government for Colonel Robert St. Pierre and Captain Jose Santana. Their crimes were robbery and murder. If the two families had been keeping a low profile since they entered the United States, finding their names in the paper drove them into hiding. Angelica was pregnant and became hysterical. If it wasn't for Sophia, she may have taken her own life.

Known only to a handful of people, there were several secret meetings between Maximilian and the Juarez Government representative while Max was in prison awaiting his fate. The representative offered a commuted sentence and passage to Europe if Max would make a statement refuting the French invasion of Mexico and that he was duped by Napoleon. Max knew that this was a non-starter and didn't bother to respond.

Max had a visitor one evening. He was led into his jail cell in the middle of the night. The visitor's cape covered his face but Max knew the voice. He was given one last chance to receive a verdict of not guilty if he would leave the country after apologizing to the Mexican people. Max agreed to make such a statement, but it never came to fruition. His visitor had second thoughts and walked out without acknowledging Max' commitment. His fate was decided then, even before the trial.

In spite of the impression left by the newspapers in Texas, Max was found guilty and executed by a firing squad. Other generals loyal to Maximilian were executed as well. General Diaz said that he would hunt down Colonel Robert St. Pierre and Captain Jose Santana and bring them back to Mexico to stand trial. Robert broke down and cried when he learned of Max' fate. He loved the man like a brother. He blamed himself for not arguing more forcibly that Max should escape with them.

The two families left Mexico with over fifteen thousand dollars in Mexican currency, thanks to Maximilian and Jose's father. St. Pierre assumed it was Max' personal funds that he gave them; he didn't ask. They were entering a foreign country, not knowing anyone there, unsure where they were going and at a distinct disadvantage when it came to the language. They exchanged their French weaponry in Brownsville for Colt revolvers and Remington rifles for the four men. They were sure Juarez had spies in town and would find out about the weapon's exchange. When they exchanged their pesos into dollars, they were forced to take a significant discount.

Their burros had gotten them this far but they needed a different type of transportation. They sold the animals and purchased four riding mounts and four horses to pull the wagons. Though it took more money than they wished to spend, they were satisfied they made the exchange. Two days later after purchasing supplies for a month in Brownsville, they went back to the small town to the east they'd been living in for two weeks. Most of the people they came in contact within Brownsville were of Mexican descent. Everyone seemed a threat.

Once they loaded up their supplies, they decided to leave the area. Over the next week, they kept within a short distance of the Rio Grande as they moved north. It took them about a week to become adjusted to their new equipment. They slept outside under the wagons and prepared and ate all their meals in the open near the wagons They were cautious of strangers and avoided contact with anyone on their trek north.

Over the next thirty days, they continued to follow the Rio Grande River north. They were suspicious of everyone, cautious in discussing any of their itinerary and nervous when purchasing supplies in the small towns they went through. Robert felt that Juarez would send people to intercept them and they wanted to be prepared.

When they were in Mexico, they were aware of the number of raids made by the Comanche deep into the country. So far they didn't have any contact with the Native Americans, but knew they could be in jeopardy while in Comanche Territory. The Native American's influence went as far north as all of New Mexico. The two families travelled by day and sheltered the wagons in trees at night. Initially they ran into a series of wind storms that had jeopardized many a settler. But as long as they kept the Rio Grande in sight, they felt sure f their location.

The four men took six hour shifts at night. Each had been in combat and was comfortable acting as a sentry. The women managed the children and prepared most of the meals. There was no vote for leadership of the group. It was assumed by all that Robert St. Pierre would be the leader.

However, in the evening they talked over the day's events and tried to correct the errors they made. Everyone spoke and voiced their concerns. St. Pierre had taken several maps when he left Mexico and although they hadn't established a destination, they were meandering north following the river. Angelica was coming out of her depression and gave birth to a seven-pound baby boy. The two families declared a three-day break in their travels, mainly to let the new mother recuperate. They'd seen the game in the area and decided to see if they could bag some deer before they continued on. Jose and one of the Mexican bodyguards brought back two deer. They cleaned and dressed both, but had one for dinner the three nights they rested.

Initially, it was Jose Santana who suggested New Mexico. He remembered the history taught to him in school, Coronado had traveled from Mexico and set up a couple of temporary settlements in the state around 1542,

Subsequently, a hundred and fifty years later the Spanish made another foray into New Mexico and established a series of forts. Many of these were later turned into small towns. The one thing that was driving the adults in the group was to be as far from Mexico as possible; therefore they were reluctant to stay in any one place too long.

They encountered very few travelers in their first month on the road. However, that all changed one afternoon when they stopped early and set up camp on a rise with a view to the valley and river below. After screening the wagons, they started preparing dinner. That's when they saw what looked like a wind storm in the valley below. Robert got out his glasses and looked at the dust being generated below. "What do you see Robert?" Santana asked."

"There're about fifty riders moving around a hundred horses in front of them. They're heading south on this side of the river. Let's stay out of sight, put out the fire and make it a cold camp tonight." Robert handed the glasses to Santana.

"Try to keep the children as quiet as possible so they don't give away our position." Jose said. They watched for an hour until the herders and horses were out of sight.

"What do you think Jose?" Robert asked.

"I can't be sure, but I think those were Comanches with stolen horses.  We ought to double the watch tonight. I also suggest that we make an early start tomorrow to put some distance between them and us. We could get up at four and leave by five AM."  Robert nodded his head in agreement.

The next day they stayed about five miles east of the river, as they travelled. They wanted to distance themselves from any Comanche that could be catching up to the group running the horses. Around noon they stopped for lunch and saw smoke coming over the next rise. They were curious and after lunch, they rode to a small hill overlooking the smoke. They could see a ranch with several outbuildings that were on fire. Robert and Jose decided to investigate, leaving the two bodyguards with the women and children.

There were seven bodies lying on the ground with either arrows in them or hatchet marks maiming the bodies. The two men checked each body; all were dead. Two were children and one was a woman, who was completely naked A couple of dogs with arrows in them lay nearby.

Jose looked in all the buildings while Robert kept lookout. They didn't find anyone alive. If there had been any stock, it'd been taken, possible by the Comanche they saw next to the river. This was their first experience to the brutal western part of the United States.

They assumed a group surprised the people on the ranch, killed them and stole their horses. There were enough corrals to handle at last a hundred horses. Jose continued to look around while Robert went back to their wagons and explained what happened below.

"Why don't you stay here? You can see us from here. It's a gruesome site and there's no one alive. I'll leave one Mexican here. Jose, myself and one of bodyguards will bury the dead and then we can move on." There were tears in the eyes of the two women when Robert told them what happened. They understood why Robert didn't want them and the children to see what had happened.

"It was dinner time before they finished burying the dead. Robert went through the home trying to find any identification for the dead or who their relatives were. The ranch was mid sized and from what he saw of the furniture inside the buildings, the ranch was successful. There was a well and the previous owners had a lot of food stuff on hand for them and their animals. He found nothing to identify them or any heirs.

Their group decided to stop at the next town and notify the people at the general store what happened. There was a brief discussion whether they should take over the property since most of the building and corrals were in good shape. It was true that the men looked at the ranch where they stopped as a potential homestead. But the massacre scared Robert off. And then there was Sophia, who said, "the sooner we leave this place, the better off we'll be."

The next day was uneventful and they travelled a little further than normal before they stopped. Each stop was based on the defensibility of the terrain. Everyone was tired but no one complained. They were happy to be out of Mexico and they looked forward to the future. Seeing the Comanches yesterday made Robert more cautious and he had two on sentry duty with each pulling a six hour shift. They repeated this strategy for the next eight days.

One day, just as they were stopping to make camp, riders were sighted in the distance. They were close to the Rio Grande River and saw some shelter nearby. They parked the wagons within some trees and had the women and children stay under the wagons. They deployed their four men as best they could and waited.

Soon it became evident that there were six men taking their time as they approached. It was as though they were assessing the situation and developing a plan of attack. As they got nearer, Jose could see that they were a rough looking bunch and their body odor permeated the warm summer afternoon. The six didn't appear to be worried as they rode into camp and smiled at Jose, who was standing in the center of a triangle defense. "Good day. We're wondering if you have any food and water to spare?" One of the riders asked.

Jose responded in Spanish. "You can fill your canteens from our barrel over there, but we only have enough food for ourselves. I'm sorry we can't be more helpful."

The six got off their horses, looked around as though assessing the situation, filled their canteens and quickly remounted. They waved goodbye and turned to leave. As they started out of the camp, the six quickly wheeled their horses back toward Robert and his group. They immediately started firing at Jose and the other three men. But Robert and the others were prepared for such a maneuver and began firing with their colts. Three of the intruders fell to the ground and the other three rode off. Robert and the others fired their rifles at the fleeing riders, but they got away. If any of them were shot, they didn't show it.

When the shooting ended, Sophia and Angelica came out from underneath the wagon and were shocked to see the three riders lying on the ground. Robert checked all three but they were dead. Unfortunately, ,one of their bodyguards, a man named Felipe Gutteriez had been shot three times and was dead. They confiscated the three horses and saddles, the bandit's guns and ammunition and all personal belongings. The three intruders and the bodyguard were buried in the trees. Robert said some prayers in French over them. Jose, Robert and Sophia took four-hour shifts the rest of the night. They were a sad lot that started moving at five AM the next morning.

With the loss of one of their men, they had to make some changes. The women were taking care of the children, as well as preparing most of the meals. As the weeks went by, the two women began taking turns driving the wagons and the three men tried their hand at cooking half of the meals. To increase their defensive capability, the men decided to teach the two women how to shoot. They started slowly with the colts and then progressed to the Remingtons. Sophia caught on quicker than Jose's wife, so Sophia took her turn on sentry duty after a month of shooting at practice targets. Before they reached their destination, each of the women was proficient in shooting.

Another chore they started to share was hunting small game to supplement their diets. Within a month, the women became skilled enough to go out together hunting game, while the men watched the children. Initially, the remaining Mexican bodyguard, went with the wives. But after a month, they went by themselves. A variety of game wasn't available. But there were plenty of rabbits and ground squirrels. The women always bagged at least two every time they went hunting. When they each bagged a turkey one day, they entered their camp with huge smiles.

# CHAPTER 5

After their experience with the six riders, Robert initiated a defensive posture while they were travelling. The women would drive the wagons while the children would ride in the back. The three men would be in the saddle all day. One would ride about thirty yards to the east of the wagons, another would ride thirty yards in front and the third in the back at the same distance. The river to their west would be used as their western marker. The object was not to be caught by surprise.

They'd run into small towns along the route about every thirty miles. Only Jose, Angelica and Fernando were fluent in Spanish. However, the other two adults and Robert's oldest boy, Rene could understand and speak some of the language. But it was normally Jose and Fernando who'd go into the town and purchase supplies. The others would remain about two hundred yards away and be alert to any problem. Jose would ask the merchants in the small towns about any sightings of the Comanche and what were the most favorable destinations to settle in.

Some named Santa Fe but most liked the town of Albuquerque. Everyone kept track of the Comanche and their recent raids. The latest was twenty miles west of the town where they stopped. Three settlers were killed and some of the livestock taken..

Three months later they saw the town of Albuquerque in front of them and camped out along the Rio Grande River which they'd been using as a navigational aide to get here. The following day Jose and Robert went to the local land office to look at the county maps and see what was for sale. They found a five hundred acre parcel five miles north of town. The previous owners were the Fergusons.

"Why did they leave?" Robert asked the land agent?"

"They came from back east and after a couple of Comanche raids on their livestock and their oldest son being killed, they decided to go back home."

This was the size that the adults said would fit their needs, so they went back to where the others were waiting and told them about the parcel and why the previous owners left. The women were reluctant to look at the parcel. "What if they come back?" Sophia asked.

"Then we tell them to leave or we'll kill them>"

"I don't like all this killing. Maybe we need to find a place that's more settled and less violent." Sophia responded.

After about an hour of discussion, they all agreed to ride to the plot of land and camp there for five days and see if that's what they all wanted.. The land had access to the river and from what the land sales office said, there was a usable well on the property, which they found. They tested the water and found that it was drinkable. With potential irrigation from the river, they could grow crops and raise livestock. There were two corrals in fairly good shape, a small barn and a two bedroom home. They could see a two acre area that had been previously cultivated. Before they left, they looked at how they could defend it against the Comanche and any others that bore them harm. All the adults voted including Fernando; it was unanimous. They would make an offer on the property.

They went back to town and bought the parcel for twelve hundred and fifty dollars, stored up on supplies for at least a month and purchased a load of lumber. They set up the wagons on the new parcel, after unloading them and started building a second home. None of the adults had ever built anything. The owner of the lumber yard showed them plans for a house and gave them many suggestions on how to proceed. He also suggested how they could enlarge the existing home.

Robert and his family took the existing home. Jose and his family would have the second house which they immediately started to build. In the interim, Jose and Angelica would use the wagons. Their furniture would be housed in the barn during construction.

Over the next six months, they experienced very little rain, many dust storms and few visitors. They were reluctant to leave the farm but after six months, two of the adult men went to Santa Fe with the buckboard to purchase more lumber for the second home and a new outbuilding.

The number of raids by the Comanche in New Mexico decreased, but the small bands in the area were hungry and relied on stealing from the small ranches. There were two raids on their farm but the Indians stayed away from the house.

Mostly, they stole vegetables from the garden. Ten armed Comanche came one afternoon and demanded food and horses. Rather than panic, Robert, Jose and Fernando stationed themselves around the ten with their rifles out, while the women inside the house trained their rifles on the riders. Jose talked to them in Spanish. "If you want food, we can help you. If you want to steal from us, we'll kill all of you." He cocked his rifle and aimed it at the lead Comanche.

The Comanche looked at each other and the well armed group around them. The leader said they were hungry and wouldn't steal if they could have food and water. Robert went into the house and brought out some biscuits, potatoes and corn. He also led the chief to the store house and showed him a quarter of a steer that was aging. He pointed to the meat and two of the Comanche lifted it off the hook and the ten left after they watered their horses at the trough. "Do you think we accomplished anything?" Sophia asked Robert as she stepped out onto the porch..

"None of us were killed or shot and we didn't give up much. Let's see what they do in the future."

The Comanche came periodically asking for food and water. Robert felt it was a small price to pay to keep them from raiding the farm. While they were working on the main house one day, they had visitors with some stock to sell. Ten Comanche brought twenty head of cattle. Again, it was left to Jose to bargain with them. They bought the cattle for two hundred dollars, though the asking price was much higher. Jose asked them if they could bring them a bull. This was the start of their trading with the Comanche. Jose didn't ask where the stock came from, but the people on the farm no longer feared a raid by these Indians.

They rigged up some temporary containment before supper.. By the next evening they had a corral that would hold the additional twenty cattle. The following day they bought enough hay from one of the neighboring farms and built enclosures for the hay and added two more corrals.

One of the women at a neighboring farm had been a school teacher. They met her and her husband at the general store in Albuquerque and started talking, and learned that she was fluent in languages. They asked if she could come and teach everyone at the ranch. She came once a week to teach everyone English. The children caught on quicker than the adults, but with all eight practicing with each other, they soon were able to converse in English. Prior to this everyone spoke French and Spanish.

Within a month, the Comanche returned with ten cows and an older bull. In the interim, the three men had cultivated about five acres near the river and set about planting hay. After a year, they were able to grow enough hay to feed their cattle. The bull did his job and after two years they sold enough cattle to break even. The Comanche sold them some wild horses that Jose and Fernando were able to break and sell to neighboring farms and ranches. After five years they were making money and Fernando married a local woman. The three men built him and his new wife, Lupe,  a home Their complex now contained three homes, a barn, five corrals, a hay field, a garden and two buildings used to store food and hay.

One day, about five years from the time they arrived, Jose and Fernando, the former bodyguard, were in Albuquerque, buying supplies for the group. When they were finished they decided to have a beer at the local tavern. There were about ten people in the small one room bar. Most were cowboys from the neighboring ranches that they knew, but there were three men that stood out from the rest. Jose could hear them conversing in Spanish and he recognized the dialect. It was from the Mexico City area. He didn't engage them but every once in a while the three would look in his direction and then talk among themselves.

"I think we better leave Fernando. I don't like the way those three are looking us over." Jose paid for the beers, left the saloon and the two rode toward their farm. About a half mile from the saloon, Jose signaled Fernando to follow him into some heavy growth.. "I'd like to see if they follow us. I don't like the way they looked us over."

They waited fifteen minutes and sure enough, the three newcomers were following the path that Jose and Fernando had taken. "What do you want to do?" Fernando asked.

"Let's follow them at a distance. I want to see what they have in mind. I'd like to alert Robert but we can take them if necessary."

They stayed out of sight and tracked the three riders to within two hundred yards of their complex and watched them as they trained binoculars on the farm. After thirty minutes, the Mexicans retraced their steps and headed back toward Albuquerque. Jose and Fernando waited until they were sure they weren't coming back and then headed to the farm.

Everyone thought they were free of the past. Initially, they thought Juarez or Diaz would send someone to bring them back, mainly because they were so close to Maximilian I. As the years went by, the group forgot about Juarez and went about trying to make the farm a success. When he heard the news, Robert was distraught and Sophia broke down and cried. "It's been over five years since we left Mexico. Why now? Sophia sobbed.

What do you want to do?" Robert asked the others.

"It would be easy to do nothing, but I don't like the odds. They can bring more men than we're capable of handling. I say the three of us go and take them out." Jose was firm.

"What do you mean take them out?" His wife asked.

"We kill them." Angelica's hand went to her mouth when she heard her husband's response.

Fernando was quiet for a moment before he responded. "This is like heaven to me and I have no intention of having it taken away from us. I say we kill them. There's no wire in the town that they could use to transmit our location."

Robert stood. "You women know what to do if we don't come back. I don't want to do this but I don't think there's any question what we should do. Let's saddle up and get this done." He looked at Jose and Fernando.

They assumed they'd meet up with the three strangers in Albuquerque, but just in case, they took extra ammunition, another horse and a three days supply of food and water. "We're not going to just rush in; we're going to take this slow and be sure we're protected at all times." Robert said.

They left at four in the afternoon and were in the town within forty-five minutes. They checked in the saloon to see if the three were there and then at the small hotel. Only Robert went inside the six-room inn, Jose stayed at the front door and Fernando held the horses. The clerk was at the reception desk when Robert walked up to him.

"There were three Mexicans staying here, what are their room numbers?" Robert asked the clerk.

"We don't give out information on our guests," was the response.

Robert put his colt on the desk in front of the clerk. "I don't have time to play games. Are they here or not?"

The eyes of the clerk gave him away. "They checked out two hours ago."

"Where did they go?"

The clerk was silent for a few seconds and probably was going to stone wall his visitor but though better of it and responded. "They checked out and headed south along the Rio Grande."

Robert smiled and put his gun back in the holster, "thank you."

When he came out of the hotel, Fernando and Jose were already in the saddle. "They checked out two hours ago and headed south along the river. Let's have a point in case they're waiting to ambush us; I'll go first, then Jose and then Fernando. And, let's assume they know we'll be coming after them." Robert said as they headed south.

Although the ground was hard and the constant wind erased most of their tracks, they found enough to know they were on the right course. As darkness fell, they decided to stop for the night, have something to eat and move on in the morning. They were hoping to close the gap on the three Mexicans.

The next morning, they found where the three Mexicans had camped last night. "Well at least were on the right route." Jose said.

About four in the afternoon they saw the three riders in the distance and then they disappeared. "Either they're making camp for the night or they spotted us and are setting up a trap." Fernando was agitated.

"If they know where we are and they know we're chasing them, they have the advantage. We need to do something that reverses that advantage." Robert said as they stopped near the river.

"What do you suggest?" Jose asked.

"It's a bold move, but we could ride all night and get ahead of them." Robert said to the other two.

"How do we do that Robert, since we don't know the area?" Fernando asked.

"We know it better than they do; remember we came this way five years ago. The land is pretty flat. We can head due east for two hours and then turn directly south. Well ride south until one AM and then turn west toward the river. The stars are out and we can use the North Star for navigation. We'd have to take it slow, but I bet we can get a couple of miles ahead of them. It also might neutralize any thought they might have about attacking us tonight."

Initially, the terrain was rough and they had to walk their horses, but after making the turn south, they were more comfortable. Other than Fernando's horse stumbling one time, they made it back near the river by four AM and set up defensive positions.

"What if they're not after us?" Jose asked.

"When we stop them, they'll fight if they're hostile. If they don't fight, then we'll talk to them and find out what they're about." Robert replied.

Around six AM, they saw some dust north of them heading directly toward Robert and his group. The three hid behind some boulders and when the Mexicans were within rifle range,

Robert fired a couple of warning shots over their heads. "Halt, we'd like to talk to you."

The three Mexicans dove off their horses and came up in a crouch position and fired at them. Jose was by far the best shot; he shot one of the Mexicans in the heart; the man fell over dead.

The other two Mexicans tried to run for some rocks but Hernando dropped one of them, but the third made it to cover. They traded shots but soon the one remaining Mexican was trying to wait it out, perhaps until darkness and then make a run for it. His position was such that they were reluctant to attack, because they'd be exposed. The sun was making the wait unbearable. At noon, Jose decided to try to flank the Mexican. He crawled about two hundred feet south and then made his way east where there was some cactus bushes that would give him cover. When he was behind their adversary, he yelled out in Spanish.. "We can shoot you or you can surrender."

The Mexican placed a handkerchief over the barrel of his rifle and stuck it in the air. "Don't shoot. I want to surrender." He replied in Spanish.

"Be careful. I don't like the way he's carry his rifle." Jose was watching the Mexican closely as the man deliberately approached Jose and Fernando. Robert was still behind him..

As Jose and Fernando waited for the Mexican to drop his rifle, the man slowly lowered it to the firing position. Before he could pull the trigger, Jose shot him in the head and the Mexican fell on his face and didn't move.

They went through the Mexicans' saddlebags. There was an order signed by newly elected President Diaz to hunt for and bring back Colonel Robert St. Pierre and Captain Jose Santana. They confiscated the dead men's belongings and buried the three. They were richer by three horses and saddles and one thousand Pesos. But they were poorer because the Mexican Government knew where they were and it would be a burden forever on the families.

On the way back, they decided to bypass Albuquerque in the event someone was looking for the three Mexicans. As they approached the farm, they heard the chatter of rifle fire and they raced to the gate. All the firing was coming from the main house and was directed toward ten Comanche who were hiding behind the fences. Jose rode up to the Comanche leader and asked him what was going on. "We come to sell horses and women shoot at us. Running Bird is wounded in the foot, White Squirrel wet his pants and Smiling Moon stinks."

Jose and the others tried hard not to laugh but they couldn't help it. Robert yelled into the house and told the women to come out. The three women, still holding their rifles slowly opened the front door, stepped outside and stopped on the porch. "This is as far as we'll go until those savages leave the farm."

They bought seven of the ten horses the Comanche had and traded the three saddles for the other three. Jose was the bronco buster in the group. Once the horses could be ridden, there was a ready market in the surrounding farms and ranches.

"Tell women not to shoot next time we come." The leader of the Comanche said as they rode off.

# CHAPTER 6

The first thing they did after they returned from eliminating the threat of the three Mexicans was to have a meeting with all the adults. Robert, Jose and their wives had talked it over ahead of time but it came as a surprise to Fernando and his wife, Lupe. "The three of us have been together for over five years. We do the same work, take the same risks and share the same food. It's only fair that you share what we've built here."

Fernando cried and they drank a bottle of wine or two.. In fractured English, he said "this is the happiest day of my life. I love you all."

Robert, with his new command of the English language, put the agreement in writing and all signed the document. The farm was paying for itself and the owners decided to hire three confederate veterans to do most of the bronco busting and herding of their cattle. It also gave them three more guns in case Diaz or Juarez wanted to send more men. The six males built another dwelling to house the three new employees of the farm.

The town of Albuquerque was growing. There was the usual saloon, livery stable, general store, bank, etc. The population numbered a little over two thousand and the city council was thinking of building an opera house. The current sheriff was retiring and the town threw a big party to thank him for his service. The three families on the farm went and met some of their new neighbors. The mayor asked Jose if he'd be interested in being appointed to that position. "Would I be able to have a deputy?"

"I think that can be arranged, but I'd have to run it by the city council."

His two children, Fernando and Maria were of school age and he and his wife were spending more time in the city. Jose was interested; he talked it over with Fernando and asked him if he'd be interested in being his deputy; he said yes.

But since it would take time away from the farm, Jose wanted to talk it over with the other two families. "I'd be gone every other week and Fernando would stay here. I'd come back and Fernando would go into town. I won't take the job if anyone here is against it." Robert smiled and told Jose to accept the job. "With the three new workers, we can handle it."

Up until now they've been sharing expenses and income. Over the past year, each had withdrawn an equal amount from the joint bank account for their personal use. "This will also bring in additional money for all of us. We have four children of school age and Lupe is expecting."

"Sharing has worked so far, but I think this is something you and Fernando will earn separate from the farm and should be yours." Robert countered.

"Since we'll be gone half the month, someone has to pick up the work we don't do during those two weeks. I think we should give the farm half of what we earn. That seems fair to me. Fernando suggested.

They took a vote and it was unanimous. Jose accepted the position, conditioned on Fernando being his deputy. The city council agreed to have Fernando serve as deputy. They also provided the sheriff a home in town. It was ideal because Fernando and Jose alternated being in town a week at a time.

Most of the crime involved the Crazy Mary Saloon. On Saturday night someone always got drunk and a fight started. Fernando and Jose, whoever was in town, would get up, lock up the culprit and let him go the next day after paying a fine. There was an occasional theft of someone's horse or the rustling of a couple of cows, but for the most part there was very little crime. For two years most crimes in the area were kept in check by the local ranchers.

One night six men rode into Albuquerque at midnight, broke down the rear door to the bank and used dynamite to open the safe. Fifteen thousand dollars was taken. Fernando heard the explosion, quickly dressed and ran toward the sound. As he came down the main street, six men mounted their horses and rode toward him. "Stop or I'll shoot" He yelled.

At least two of the riders fired at him and he was shot in the right leg, left shoulder and right side of his chest; he fell in the dirt, bleeding from all his wounds.. The riders rode east. Two of the townspeople came to Fernando's aid and carried him the doctor's office. It was no use, the deputy was beyond help; he'd lost too much blood. Lupe heard the shooting and ran out as the riders made their way out of town. She was at his side when he passed away. The mayor sent for Jose and within three hours a posse was formed and ten men rode after the bandits. Robert and one of their confederate workers joined the posse.

Angelica and Sophia came in a wagon to pick up the body of Fernando. Lupe cried and looked to the two women for some answers. "We'll take him back to the farm and bury him there. You still own one third of the farm and can live there as long as you want." Sophia and Lupe were close and Robert's wife put her arm around Lupe's waist and helped her into the wagon.

The posse narrowed the lead the bank robbers had but, the hills were in sight and Jose knew they had to catch them soon or they'd either lose them in the dark or the posse might be victims of a trap.

For some reason the robbers decided to make a stand in the foothills and it was only a matter of time. Jose sent three of his deputies to the right and three to the left of the bandit's position, trying to flank them. While he was concentrating his fire directly at the robbers, the six who were surrounding the bandits set up a pincer movement that required the bandits to leave their position and become exposed to fire from all sides. Still, the shooting continued for nearly an hour. Around midnight, a white flag appeared from the bandits and someone on their side said they'd like to give up.

Jose shouted back, "thrown out all your weapons."

After they threw out their weapons, all six bandits walked toward Jose. The former Mexican Captain had been in conflict several times. One thing he learned from a superior officer was not to give away an advantage too soon. Wait until the enemy commits and cannot turn the tables on you, was what he was taught. "Hold your positions men. Keep your rifles pointed at the six until they're on the ground." Jose shouted.

Jose yelled out to the six robbers to stop, get on their knees and put their hands behind their head. The six continued moving toward Jose and his posse. Jose fired at the closest bandit and hit him in the shoulder; the bandit fell to the ground. 'We'll keep firing at you until you drop all your weapons, get on your knees and put your hands behind your head. If you don't do it now, we'll start firing at you. We're covered; you're not."

Jose told his people to stay behind cover and he fired at the feet of another robber and all five got on their knees, threw away their concealed weapons and put their hands behind their head. Members of the posse frisked them and each still had a handgun on their person. They found the money taken from the bank in one of the robber's saddlebags. Several members of the posse asked Jose why he suspected the robbers still had their weapons. "I had that tactic pulled on me years ago. My commander stopped me from making a complete fool of myself and perhaps getting my men killed."

When they rode into town at dawn with the bandits in handcuffs, the town's people clapped. Some in the crowd yelled, "get a rope. We don't need a judge."

Jose fired his rifle in the air to get everyone's attention. "There will be no lynching. If anyone tries to take the law into their hands, I'll shoot them. Fernando was a close friend of mine, but I still want these men tried in a court." The townspeople dispersed.

The roving judge was scheduled the following week. Robert and one of their confederate employees decided to stay in town until the trial. With Jose's deputy murdered by the bandits, no one was sure if some would still try to take the law into their hands and break the killers out of jail and hang them. Fernando's body had been taken back to the farm by Sophia and

Angelica. Lupe was distraught and needed the women. Sophia told her that everything would be okay. She repeated that Lupe was still one third owner in the farm and could stay as long as she wanted.

Since he lost his deputy, Jose asked the three former confederates at the farm if they had any training in law enforcement. One of the confederates had served as a military policeman for a year before he fought at the battle of Appomattox. His name was Frank Wilson and he agreed to be Jose' deputy. Jose again asked permission from the other two families on the farm if it was okay to use one of the confederates as his deputy; both families and Lupe said it was okay. After a week of orientation, Frank was able to take up his duties and spell Jose every other week.

The trial was held in the Crazy Mary Saloon. It was the largest space in the town and people came from as far away as fifty miles to see what would happen to the six bandits. Though Jose never established who killed Fernando, all six were tried for the crime of murder and found guilty. The jury sentenced all six to hang. The town didn't have a gallows, so it took an extra week to build one and bring in someone to handle the execution. The trial brought in a hundred people but the hanging brought in three hundred to view the spectacle.

Over the next two years, the group headed by Robert added another worker. This time it was a former slave from Mississippi. In spite of the civil war he and the other three confederates got along fine. Lupe ended her grieving and married one of the confederate soldiers named George Martin; he moved into her house and adopted her son.

None of the Mexicans came looking for them over the next few years, but a recession hit the area and several of their neighbors were experiencing hard times. There was constant cattle rustling in the area and they'd been raided twice. In each case they reacted quickly and recovered their stock and hung the culprits. However, one night they were raided and lost six head of cattle. Robert was positive the brother and two sons of the man they hung for cattle rustling paid them back. No one would talk and neither Robert nor Jose could prove anything. Subsequently, the brother came to the farm and threatened Jose. "My brother was a good man. I'll get you for this when you least expect it." The man said.

"I thought you already did." Robert responded.

One of the confederate soldiers working at their farm went into town on a Saturday night two weeks later and was hung by persons unknown while he was riding back to the farm. Jose investigated by going around to the ranches in the area and questioning the troublemakers in the city All he and Robert could do was wait and see if the brother and/or his nephews got drunk some night and let a few things slip.

Things were so bad financially that the three families were forced to sell most of their horses and cattle to keep afloat. Their hay crop suffered from seasonal drought; yet they survived and their losses were small in comparison to the other ranches in that area of New Mexico.

It took nearly a year but finally the rains came. They lost all their savings during the drought and but for Jose's and the confederate's income and a loan that Robert negotiated in Santa Fe, they would've lost everything.

Only one of the confederate soldiers was still with them. One had been hung, possibly by a neighbor, another married Lupe, and the third wanted to do something else and just left.. The former slave was still with them and was looked upon as family. Rene and Armand St. Pierre were young men and Fernando and Maria Santana were teenagers. Lupe's son was in school.

# CHAPTER 7

For the past fifteen years, Robert, Jose and their families felt the Mexicans were coming for them. Even as the years went by, they didn't feel safe. They tried to make the farm as defensive as possible without destroying the beauty of everything they built. There were no trees within eye distance. They hadn't planted any for fear that an intruder would use them as an offensive position.

Rain had come ending the five year drought and their horse and cattle herds increased, mainly through the efforts of their new friends, the Comanche.. Their power and destruction had ended and most Indians had to work with the white man in order to survive. They still brought horses and cattle to the farm and bargained well; they'd become businessmen. The neighbor who they believe had killed one of their workmen sold his small ranch; he and his nephews moved to Texas.

The defensive measures they instituted would be able to withstand as many as eight or nine adversaries but if more came they would have a hard time surviving unless they were lucky.

Jose, who was still sheriff, had notified two of the towns to the south to be on the lookout for Mexican Nationals. They could be dressed as soldiers, policemen or cowboys. Robert remembered that General Diaz never gave up. He hated Maximilian I, Robert and Jose. When Max was killed by the firing squad, Diaz swore that Robert and Jose would be next. When General Lopez turned on Maximilian I and left the main gate open so Diaz could enter, the two families had no choice but to run.

Recently, Robert purchased the latest rifles and new six shot Colt Paterson revolvers. Everyone on the farm was a good shot and they practiced weekly. They put up concrete walls in ten locations around the main house. Rather than have stark concrete around the house, they decorated then with flowers and ivy.

The plan was to have defensive positions for the six men living on the farm. The three women, Fernando Santana the sixteen year old son of Jose and his younger sister, Maria would be bunkered in the main house. Rene and Armand St. Pierre, who were twenty-three and twenty-one respectively, would take defensive positions outside with Robert, Jose, Lupe's husband and the former slave, if there was an attack.

The message came from one of the towns on the Texas and New Mexico border. There were fifteen of them traveling with three pack animals. They were expected within five days. Hopefully Jose and Robert would be ready. Chores would be kept to a minimum and defensives checked daily. The mayor in Albuquerque knew the situation and granted Jose and his deputy some time off from their jobs as sheriff and deputy; the previous sheriff agreed to fill in for a short time. It was Robert who saw them first and told the others to take their positions.

The Mexicans immediately surrounded the main house where the women and children were. The attackers started firing with their rifles from all four quadrants as soon as they were within rifle range. This exposed those who were behind the concrete slabs. The confederate soldier married to Lupe was hit in the initial volley and Robert ran from his position and dragged him inside the main house, where Maria tended to his right shoulder wound. The other five defenders retreated to the main house and took up positions by the windows.

Although he was shot in the right shoulder, the confederate was able to fire with his left hand after he was attended to. The Mexicans continued their heavy fire until dark. They changed their tactics after that and every two hours they'd fire on the main house just to let them know they were outside and to keep the defenders awake. This caused stress among the three women and the children. Robert and Jose decided to balance the odds. After midnight after the most recent volley, they slipped out of the house and crawled one hundred yards west using the corrals as cover. They wanted to come up behind any of the attackers.

They saw three men sitting by a small fire, drinking either coffee or something else. Both Jose and Robert were skilled in sneaking up on adversaries. Using knives, they had no problem neutralizing the three, taking their weapons and returning to their home without being seen by the other twelve Mexicans. Though they didn't even the odds, they eliminated a good portion of the attackers and perhaps better than that, they planted a seed among the Mexicans that they weren't invincible.

The firing continued at daybreak but the defenders never saw any of their assailants. They remained in the house behind solid wooden walls that were built to repel any invaders. This went on for a day and when darkness fell only random shots were fired at them; both sides were frustrated. The Mexicans couldn't get close enough to attack the house while the defenders were outgunned, out manned and reluctant to initiate an attack.

Robert and Jose had some experience when it came to defending a position. What their adversaries didn't know was that they had a plan to take the offensive. Around eight AM, ten of the Mexicans rode past the main house where the defenders were. They started to circle the home firing their rifles at the windows similar to attacks made famous by the Comanche Indians. They were encouraged when there was only token response from inside the main home.

After the previous attack by the three Mexicans ten years earlier, Robert and Jose developed an escape plan should another attack come. While the Mexicans were concentrating their attack on the main house, Robert, Jose and the former slave sneaked out of the house via a tunnel the men built and finished five years earlier. They exited about one hundred yards from the house, covered over the exit and crawled fifty yards back until they were in position twenty yards apart. When Robert gave the signal, they fired on the ten riders killing five immediately. When their men started falling, the

Mexicans galloped away from the house. Two more of their men were shot as they were escaping and fell from their horses.

As the Mexicans were escaping, Robert and the other two ran to their corrals, quickly saddled their horses and went after the Mexicans. Robert and his group were not aware that two of the Mexicans had been wounded and that's why they didn't join the attack. It was Jose that spotted the camp and without losing their momentum, the three rode directly at the invaders firing as they raced toward them. The three Mexicans who'd been on the raid were off their horses and appeared to be breaking camp. The wounded were trying to help the other three.

The shooting from Robert and the others was so intense, that two of the Mexicans were shot and fell to the ground. The other three dropped their weapons and raised their hands. Jose, as acting sheriff, put them under arrest and made them bury the two at their camp and the others killed during the attacks. The former slave wanted to kill the three. "If you arrest them, they're going to have a trial and Mexico will get involved; Juarez and Diaz will know where we are. What's to stop the Mexicans from sending more people until we're all dead? I'm sorry, but this is a bad decision on your part. Robert, can't you talk some sense into Jose?"

"Well I'm going to kill them." The former slave named Walter Styles went up behind one of the Mexicans and took out his revolver. Jose acted quickly and knocked the gun from the man's hand. Robert reacted almost as fast and put his arms around the black man from behind and held him tightly until he calmed down

"I'm the sheriff. If I do what you say, then I'm no better than these assassins." Jose responded, but he was looking at Robert.

"As much as I want to kill them, I'm going to agree with Jose." Robert said.

"This is a bad decision on your part. I say we kill them. No one will know the difference." Walter was very upset and rode back to their compound.

When the women heard what happened they went with Walter and asked Jose what he was going to do. "I'm the sheriff. I must uphold the law and arrest them and see that they get a fair trial."

"I'm against needless killing, but you let them go, won't the Mexican Government know about the trial?" Sophia was the strong one of the two women and she continued questioning Jose.

"That's probably true."

"This is The second time they came. They'll send more won't they?"

"I also think that's true, but my conscience won't let me arbitrarily kill them. They must have their day in court."

Jose put the three in jail in Albuquerque and after taking statements from Robert and Walter, he charged the four with attempted murder.

The city appointed an attorney for the four Mexicans and his first step was to notify the Mexican Consul General in Santa Fe of the charges. A representative of the Mexican Government came to Albuquerque and petitioned to have the four released and returned to Mexico where they'd stand trial before a jury of their piers. His rationale was that the four wouldn't receive a fair trial in New Mexico.

When his petition was denied by local authorities, he hired a well known American attorney who spoke Spanish.

Before the trial started, The Mexican Government filed a writ of habeas Corpus and demanded that the American Government turn over Robert St. Pierre and Jose Santana to them. They were wanted for crimes against the people of Mexico. The specific charges dealt with their intent to steal from the country by setting up a puppet government headed by Maximilian I. They were also charged with stealing fifty thousand Pesos worth of gold from the Mexican people

The trial of the four Mexicans started and it drew people in the United States from as far away as Santa Fe and Houston Texas. There was also a significant contingent from Mexico. The trial got underway with Jose, Robert and the former confederate testifying for the prosecution. Jose covered the initial unwarranted attack and the last attack. Apparently one of the surviving Mexican Soldiers understood English and Walter Styles was questioned about his intent to kill the three survivors.

As it turned out, Styles was the best witness for the prosecution. When asked why he wanted to kill the survivors, after they'd surrendered? He clearly stated, "If we didn't kill them, the Mexican Government would get involved, which they did, and Juarez and Diaz would know exactly where we are and who's left. Nothing would prevent them from sending more raids until they succeeded. If the survivors are dead, they probably wouldn't risk another raid."

The defense attorney tried to cloud the issues by questioning Robert and Jose about the charges that they used their position in the Maximilian Government to steal money from the Mexican Treasury. The prosecution objected each time and the judge told the jury to disregard the accusations because they had nothing to do with the attack in the State of New Mexico.

The prosecutor asked for the death penalty. While the jury was deliberating, the judge called both attorneys into his chambers. When everyone was seated, the judge showed them a telegram from the US Secretary of State. In essence, the telegram stated that Mexico and the United States made an agreement to hand the three Mexicans over to their government in return for waving the charges against Robert St. Pierre and Jose Santana in Mexico. In addition, the Mexican Government promised not to make any further attempts to capture or lure the two named individuals to Mexico. Jose objected to the prosecutor but he told Jose that his hands were tied and that the Governor wanted the trial to go away.

After the trial ended, the families on the farm had a meeting in the main house. "Robert, do you believe that Diaz and the Mexican Government will honor their agreement and leave us alone?" Angelica asked.

"I don't believe it for a second. They'll figure out a way to circumvent that agreement and come after us again. Maybe they won't come for a year or two, but they'll come. Diaz is a spiteful person."

"What should we do?" Sophia, Robert's wife asked.

"I don't know. This has been our home for around twenty years. We're respected in the community and Jose has been the sheriff for over ten years and I don't see him being voted out of office. The Mexicans are really after Jose and me. It doesn't seem fair that the two of us are bringing this trouble to all of you."

"Dad, if we leave, won't they find us wherever we go?" Rene, the son of Robert asked.

"That's a fair statement. We need to think about this hard and come to a joint decision."

"I told you we should have killed the three. You and your holier than thou attitude got us into this. If you killed them as I wanted and even tried to do, they'd think twice about coming again. "The slave known as Walter Styles was looking directly at Jose when he spoke.

# CHAPTER 8

The discussions were continuous, lengthy, a little heated, and nothing was accomplished. .Lupe and her new husband didn't want to sell and move on. Robert was adamant that the Mexicans would come again with more attackers. Jose could see both sides but was leaning toward Robert's position. He remembered Diaz as a formidable and unrelenting opponent. The man had a vendetta against him and Robert. Their sin was escaping and not being shot by a firing squad as Maximilian I was.

The three couples who owned the farm generally made all the decisions. However, Robert's two sons were in their twenties and felt they had a voice in the decision; neither wanted to move. In fact, they welcomed the Mexicans coming again. "We've beaten them twice; there's no reason why we shouldn't prevail again." Rene told the others.

The one who didn't have a vote but who was very interested in what would become of him was Walter Sykes, the former slave. "If you sell, what happens to me? I've spent the last ten years with all of you, but I have no interest in the property and therefore no vote in its disposition."

"What is it that you want?" Robert asked.

"This is the first home I've ever had. I want to be with people that want me, a place where I want to stay and a place to live out my life."

"I'm sorry that we haven't addressed your needs. It was thoughtless of us and should be addressed. Let me give it some thought." Robert responded.

There was no doubt that their five-hundred-acre farm was valuable and several buyers were interested. What made Lupe and her husband finally agree to sell was the promise that Jose extracted from the city council in Albuquerque. Lupe's husband would be hired to replace Jose as Sheriff of Albuquerque. He'd been Jose's deputy for at least seven years and the townspeople liked him. In addition, the ex-slave was offered a position by the new owners from Santa Fe to work on the farm.

It seemed like a win-win situation for all. However, the grown children really had no choice. They either went with their family or they could be hired hands for the new owners. And then there was Walter Sykes. He thought it over after meeting the new owners and said he didn't want to work for them. He asked Robert if there were any other options for him.

There was an option that Robert hadn't thought of until Rene said to him, "why don't you take him with us. Everyone likes him; he's a good worker and he wants a home. Why can't he live with us?"

"It may take us some time before we find what we're looking for. How do we pay him?"

"Dad, he wants a home and he wants to be with people he likes and who like him. Tell him straight out and see what he says."

It took nearly a month to inventory, establish a price for the animals and supplies and complete the paperwork When the reconciliation was complete, the three families each received one third of the amount collected. Lupe and her husband moved to Albuquerque and lived in the sheriff's house. Lupe's husband hired one of the freighters in town as his deputy. Armand and Rene looked for jobs but there wasn't anything that suited them, so they were leaning toward the option of going with their parents.

Walter Sykes accepted Robert's proposal to come with the two families. He had the biggest smile on his face when Robert made him the offer. The three families kicked in fifty dollars each and gave it to Walter for all his help during his time with the three families.

Rene had been seeing one of the daughters of a neighboring farm family. He decided to talk over the move with her and see if she had any advice. He really didn't know how much he liked her and he wanted to see what her feelings were. They hadn't been intimate yet; her mother kept warning her to stay a virgin or she'd lose a lot of her allure. It was a two hour ride on horseback to their farm; he got there around dinner time. Her mother asked Rene to stay for dinner. He gratefully accepted.

Fred and Helga Curtiss were from Alabama and had been in the area for ten years. Rene was a handsome young man with good manners and seemed like a good catch for a young woman, but there was something that he didn't know until he asked her if she wanted to marry him. It was after dinner when he made his pitch "I was hoping your brother would ask me." Kathleen Curtiss said and Rene's ardor cooled immediately.

"You mean I've been coming over here for nothing. What a dummy. Armand is going to get a big laugh out of this."

Rene hopped on his horse and rode home. He didn't even thank the mother for the nice dinner. He played Kathleen's answer over and over until he got home. When he told Armand what happened, his brother laughed. "I've hardly spoken to her and I sure as hell don't want to get married to some farm girl. I'm going with mom and dad."

It didn't end there. Armand laughed every time he and Rene got together. "Did you even bed her?" Armand was smaller than Rene but a lot faster. Rene had a hard time catching his brother. They ended up in a wrestling match that Sophia tried to break up. "What's up boys? I've never see you act this way before." Both Armand Rene burst out laughing and Sophia walked off in a huff.

Robert, Jose and their families didn't tell anyone where they were going. Though they all had command of the English, French and Spanish languages, they didn't know anyone well enough to visit or ask advice where they should relocate. On a day in May, the two families, Walter, a couple of extra horses, six cows and two wagons filled with furniture left their beloved farm and started out toward Santa Fe.

Robert's two children, Rene and Armand were twenty three and twenty one respectively. They were both five foot ten inches tall; Rene was heavier. Both were taller than their father. Jose's children, Fernando and Maria were sixteen and fifteen. The daughter was going to be a beauty and Fernando was already six feet tall. All four children were experienced in firing rifles and handguns. The two families were very close and comfortable that they could handle any adverse situation. They liked having Walter along. He kept them entertained as he told them about his life as a slave and how they used to get the best of their overseer. Everyone would look forward to dinner, when Walter would tell his tall tales.

The first and second night out on their way to Santa Fe, they stopped along a small creek, took baths and had a nice dinner. Rene, the oldest of the four children on the trip had some questions for the four adults. He, most of all, had not accepted that they had to leave their home. "Why are we being forced to leave our home? The Mexicans said in court documents, that they wouldn't pursue us anymore."

"The Mexican Government sent two groups to eliminate us. The four of us don't believe them. We believe they'll try again. We know that Juarez and Diaz want to put an end to any thought of foreign rule. We're the last piece of the puzzle and he intends to have us shot before a firing squad. Jose and I've met them both, dealt with both and actually fought against both. We know them well, you do not." Robert responded.

"All they want is the gold you took when you left the country. Why don't you give it back and make peace with them." Rene responded.

Robert was quick to respond. "Where did you get such nonsense?"

"I was at the hearings and I know enough Spanish to understand what they were saying. Their lawyer said the Mexican Government wanted the money you stole."

Jose jumped into the conversation. "We didn't take anything from the country, no gold, no artifacts and no currency. The money we had to buy the land and get through the first five years in New Mexico came from Maximilian and my father. We knew there was looting going on in the last days of the conflict, but we didn't have any part in that. If there was any gold taken and I don't say I believe the Mexicans, then Generals Marquez or Lopez could have been the ones. It wasn't us."

"Why didn't you tell us this before?" Rene asked.

"What was there to tell? Were we supposed to tell our four children that we didn't take anything? General Diaz hated the Emperor and consequently since both Robert and myself were very close to the Emperor, we were fair game. Rene, have you ever seen any gold anywhere on the farm or in the houses? How about the two Wagons or our saddlebags? If you think we stole gold from the Mexicans then what gold is left ought to be there. Maybe you'd like to search us personally or look in the wagons. If we had it, that's where I would look." Jose's face was red and he was angry. Angelica put her arm around him and tried to get him to calm down.

"Dad and Jose, I'm sorry I accused you. I shouldn't have taken what the Mexicans said as the truth. Diaz may have lied to the attackers. But I still don't believe we had to leave our home."

"Rene, we've had this discussion many times before. The decision is made. Live with it. If you want, I'll give you a reasonable amount of money to get started on your own, wherever you choose." Robert looked directly at his son.

"No. I just wanted to voice my opinion and I let my mouth run away with me. I'm committed to going with the rest of you and starting over. I'll never raise this issue again and I apologize to everyone."

Their third night out was more adventuresome. The winds came up and they had to stop early and find a sheltered position for the wagons and livestock. The wind was so strong that it was dangerous to start a fire. Around four in the afternoon, they were visited by two strangers, who claimed they got lost in the dust storm, blown up by the strong winds. They asked for food and some shelter until they were able to move on. The families fed the two men and in return had them do a few chores to pay for the hospitality.

Around two in the morning, Jose heard some noises near the horses. They'd been hearing coyotes the last two nights; and initially assumed they were near their livestock. But the more he listened, he became alarmed. He grabbed his rifle and woke Rene and told him about the noise. The two made their way toward the animals. That's when they saw a shadow approaching the horses.

Jose yelled out to the individual to stop and back up slowly. A shot rang out and a bullet hit the tree near Jose's head. He dropped to a knee, but Rene got off a shot and the shadow cried out in pain and fell to the ground. They heard a horse behind them gallop out of camp and although they fired at the fleeing horse and rider, he didn't stop.

The shadow they saw near the horses was one of the men who asked for shelter yesterday; he was dead. Rene checked but the other man who came with the dead intruder was gone. He'd taken his horse and some food. They buried the dead man, confiscated his horse and saddle, broke camp early the next morning and moved toward Santa Fe.

The hub of New Mexico during this time was famous for the Santa Fe Trail and for being a significant cultural center. Its history went back to the Indian Tribes that lived here around 1,100 and disappeared about two hundred years before Coronado explored the area in 1540. It's the oldest Capitol in the United States and was established around 1607, long before the English settlement in Jamestown. The Spanish Provisional Government Capitol for their territory in the United States was in Santa Fe. The influence of early native tribes and the Spanish permeated the entire town. The Palace of the Governors was the main building in town. It was one of the oldest buildings in New Mexico and was located at the east end of the town square. Its architecture was Spanish but the décor was Native American

They still had no idea where they planned to settle, but they camped outside the town and stayed a month trying to determine which way they should travel. They'd worked hard the past twenty plus years trying to survive and raise their families. This was vacation time and where better than Santa Fe.

They visited all the historical sites in the area, ate the rich Spanish and Indian Cuisine and spent their leisure time riding around the area. After considerable soul-searching, the two families decided to go to California.

# CHAPTER 9

During their time in Albuquerque, the transcontinental railroad had been completed. Yet, none of the nine traveling to San Francisco had ever been on a train. They were apprehensive until they went over the mountains. Thereafter, they settled down and enjoyed the view of the western part of the United States. Prior to leaving Santa Fe, they sold their horses, cattle, and wagons in Santa Fe. Angelica was heartbroken that Jose said she had to sell her furniture that had been passed down from her mother. After a few tears, Jose relented and all the furniture ended up on the train to San Francisco.

The great city unnerved them when they arrived. None of them were comfortable in the hustle and bustle of this vibrant city by the sea. Jose and Robert had been young men of the world, with a gay time prior to marriage. Yet, they had trouble being comfortable in the area known as the Bowery.

Rather than give up on the great city too soon, all the adults decided to check out the city for themselves before they ruled against it. The four children went to the beach and the women went shopping with Walter escorting them. Jose and Robert met with an investment group at the San Francisco Trust Bank to invest some of the money they had realized from the sale of the farm. The investment group was able to provide some options they hadn't realized were available. By morning they completed their business and then joined their children on the beach.

The two men hadn't seen an ocean since they left Mexico and they enjoyed walking on the beach. That evening they all went to the opera. After two enjoyable weeks, they decided the city wasn't where they wanted to live. They took a steamer south and got off at the wharf in Santa Barbara. Their success as farmers in New Mexico would dictate their future endeavors.

When they went ashore, they fell in love with the beautiful location. The following month was spent looking for a place to call home; specifically, they wanted land. When they were shown a three-hundred-acre parcel in Los Alamos, they knew they found what they wanted.

Though the land on average was more expensive than in New Mexico, the number of growing seasons would more than offset the additional costs. Their new property came with two wells, a main house, a bunkhouse, a barn, storage buildings and a portion already cultivated, growing hay.

The male owner of the property died and his wife and small children were unable to work the property. She sold what livestock she had to the two families and moved back to Texas, where her family lived. Jose, Robert, Walter and the three boys took inventory, improved the corrals, holding pens and then went to work on the fencing surrounding the property. They subsequently built a second and third home. Jose was surprised that the furniture his wife cherished had been sold in San Francisco

The adjoining neighbors to the south made an unexpected visit while they were working on the new corrals, Franklin Sutter his wife and three children gave the two families an aged half steer as a housewarming gift. Two of the neighbor's children were white the third was black. The father was originally from Alabama; his wife's name was Maria and had come from Seville Spain. Sutter was surprised they had a black man with them and made a special effort to welcome the man,

"Walter is an ex-slave who's been with us over ten years. He's a part of the family." Jose Santana said.

"He seems like a very intelligent man. Where did he come from?"

"Alabama."

A month later the two families and Walter were invited to a party at the Sutter's Ranch on a Saturday afternoon. They met some of their neighbors and some people from Santa Ynez by the name of Enrique Contreras, who was Maria Sutter's brother, Silas and Marjorie Smith and Sarah and Tommy Sanchez were also in attendance. The later couple seemed to be the guests of honor at the party

Most of the guests seemed to be in awe of this couple. Robert asked several people who the Sanchez' were but all he got in return was a smile. The wine was provided by the Sanchez' winery but the beef was provided and cooked by Sutter's vaqueros over an open pit; it was outstanding. Rene and Armand were in their glory. There were many young people of their age at the party and at least three attractive young ladies that they made a point to meet. Both were talking to Henrietta Sparkman when Tommy Sanchez and his wife Sarah introduced themselves to the two young men.

Sarah Sanchez was probably the most beautiful woman they ever met but the husband was puzzling to them. He wasn't tall but he had a firm handshake and a pleasant smile; but he always seemed to be on alert. To René, the man had the eye of a hunter. He learned later that Tommy was of Sioux descent and Sarah had been married to Crazy Horse, a Sioux warrior. They owned Rancho Del Prado in Santa Ynez and had about thirteen vaqueros riding for them.

Walter was treated as a special guest by Franklin Sutter and the two could be seen taking a walk around Franklin's property. "I don't mean to be offensive, but do you have any negro blood in your family?"

"Perhaps when I get to know you better I can address your question.".

Earlier, Sarah invited Robert, Jose and their families to visit them at their ranch and have lunch next Wednesday. She smiled at them as she said, "I hope the two of you will come."

Sarah told them to take the train to Santa Ynez and they'd have a couple of their vaqueros pick them up in multiple carriages. Juan and Linda had been in Santa Barbara at the time of the Sutter's welcoming party, but they were home this week and came to the luncheon.

Tommy wasn't the least surprised that the Wellington sisters, Susanne and Margaret and their father and mother had been invited. His wife was a natural matchmaker and couldn't resist the temptation whenever the opportunity presented itself. With the arrival of Rene and Armand St. Pierre to the area, it was an opportunity. The two sisters were in their late teens and a flock of the locals were chasing after them; both were charming and attractive. Their family was in the horse business and had a ranch in Santa Ynez.

Though it rained early in the morning, it was clear by 10AM and a beautiful April day. The fare at lunch was light and Tommy introduced a new varietal. After lunch they were treated to some fancy riding by three of the vaqueros at Rancho Del Prado. It was clear that the two young St. Pierre boys took a fancy to the two Wellington sisters. Tommy looked at Sarah and she had a big smile on her face. There wasn't enough time to go fishing at the pond near to Juan and Linda's home but the invitation was made to all that when they returned, fishing would be at the top of the list of things to do..

The St. Pierre boys invited the two Wellington girls to go on a picnic near the Santa Ynez River next Saturday. The girl's parents agreed to act as chaperons. The young men took the train to Los Olivos and the parents sent a driver to pick them up and bring them to their ranch. The girls were excited. They prepared fried chicken, salad and dessert. The boys brought French wine and a loaf of bread baked by their mother, Sophia. The area they selected along the river was fairly pristine. It obviously had been used numerous times for this type of venue. Some of previous users had fashioned benches out of railroad ties.

The area wasn't all rocks; there was a spot where the grass was short. The parents had brought a croquet set with them and the girls were playing against the boys when two Spanish looking young men came up to the foursome and an argument started. "I thought the four of us were going on a picnic today." One of the Spanish young men said to the two girls.

"We didn't promise anything Roberto." Susanne replied.

"Come on guys. This is a private party. Perhaps you can discuss this with the girls at another time." Rene said to the two young Spaniards.

The taller of the two intruders struck Rene with his fist and Armand tackled the other Spaniard and a wrestling match ensued with neither side gaining an advantage. The girls' father had been enjoying a nap after a big lunch. His wife woke him and told him to come. .Eventually, he broke up the fight and asked Filipe and Jose, the two young Spaniards to leave. The two dusted themselves off and yelled challenges at Rene and Armand, but eventually they left, but not before yelling, "you're those French people who killed the guards at the border crossing in Mexico."

The fight put a damper on the outing and they packed up and returned to the Wellington's Ranch. Armand and Rene thanked the girls and their parents for the invitation and were taken to the train station in Los Olivos. "I'll tell you one thing for sure. The girls are prettier here than in Albuquerque." Armand said.

When they returned home they told their parents about the altercation with the two men. "Had you seen the two before?" Robert asked.

"No. but the Wellingtons obviously had. Armand responded.

"So they know about us. The question is who is spreading the story and what does it mean? tt sounds like you handled it well. I'm not asking you to avoid any confrontation, I'd just like to keep a low profile until were better established here." Robert said.

"No problem, we have enough to do to get this place in a profit mode. But, did you kill some border guards trying to escape Mexico?" He asked.

"We did what we had to do to protect you, your mother and Jose's wife/".

When he told Jose and Walter what happened, they were puzzled. "We've not been anywhere. The Sutter's is the only outing we've been on. I wonder if this is something that has been fed to the Spanish speaking people in the area. Well, we have to be on the alert and take care when we leave the farm not to put ourselves in a precarious position. I thought we were through with this." Jose said.

Sophia and Angelica didn't take the situation well. Both cried and Angelica wanted to sell the farm and move away. "I think we've moved for the last time. If they come, they'll wish they hadn't. Jose responded.

# CHAPTER 10

Two months after their sons got into an altercation because of the Wellington girls, their farm was raided, while the men were working in the field. Three horses were taken, several corrals were damaged and about a fourth of their fencing was cut. Some of it could've been done over a few days because of the proximity of the fencing to the main house.

Robert called on Franklin Sutter. His property bordered them on the south. After they exchanged pleasantries, Robert asked Franklin if he saw anyone unusual on either property over the past week. "Actually, I haven't. Has there been a problem?" Sutter asked.

Robert told him what happened and asked his advice. "I suggest you notify the sheriff and have them send a deputy here to look at the damage. To save you some time, I can use my telegraph at the ranch to contact Jacob Thunder and have him take care of it."

"Do you know the sheriff?"

"I was introduced to him by Tommy Sanchez. The sheriff may ask Tommy to investigate. Periodically, he serves as deputy in this area. In addition to being the fastest gun alive, he's the best tracker in the area."

"You mean he's a killer?"

"No, I mean it's uncanny how fast his reactions are. I've seen him in action and no one died. He's probably the best man I ever met and a man I consider a friend. If he reaches out to you, don't be alarmed. He's the half-breed son of Sitting Bull, the famous Sioux Chieftain. His wife is equally nice and so are her children. I believe you met Juan Sanchez, who's a prominent attorney in Santa Barbara. He and his wife Linda live near the pond on Rancho Del Prado."

Jacob Thunder knew that Tommy Sanchez was a busy man. In addition to the cattle on the ranch, about one-third was planted with grapes. That business had been thriving for the past ten years. Although he was reluctant to ask, Tommy was closer to the situation in Los Alamos than he. The wire he sent wasn't demanding; it was requested if Tommy wasn't too busy. This month was unusually busy, but when Tommy saw who one of the parties was, he didn't hesitate to respond.

Two days later Tommy Sanchez and his adopted son Juan rode up their entryway and asked to speak to Jose and Robert. "The sheriff asked me to investigate the raid on your property. My son Juan generally comes with me unless he's too busy. Why don't you tell us what happened?" Tommy asked Robert.

They looked at the corrals where the horses were taken and Tommy and Juan were able to track them a short distance. "I think we can follow these horses and see where they ended up. Maybe you'll want to come with us. We can wait until you saddle up."

Robert looked at Jose who nodded and they went back to get a couple of horses. The four took their time but they were able to follow the tracks which led to a holding pen at the livery stable in Los Alamos. While the other three were watering the horses, Tommy asked the livery stable owner who brought the four horses here.

"It was Crazy Jack Sloane and his two sons Emory and Sam."

"Where can I find them?"

The owner looked down the road. "I can see their horses at the saloon in the next block.

Be careful, they're meaner than a caged rattlesnake."

The four rode down to the saloon, tied up their horses. "Juan you go in the rear and make sure no one goes out that way. Take Robert with you. Jose and I'll go in the front and arrest the three."

Tommy waited a few minutes and when he was sure the other two had come in the back, he and Jose walked in the front. Other than the bartender, Juan, and Robert, there were three cowboys at a table near the bar. With Jose a few steps behind him, Tommy walked up to the table.

"Are you Jack Sloane and are these your two sons Emory and Sam?"

"Who wants to know?"

"I do. I'm Tommy Sanchez the deputy for this district and I'm asking?"

"Well, we're them, so what?" The father said.

"You stole three horses from the Santana and St. Pierre ranch and you're under arrest. Put your weapons on the table in front of you."

"We're not going to do any such thing and if the four of you don't leave right now, we're going to kill you. Oh, we see the two at the back door. It doesn't matter, we'll get them."

The two sons rose and looked directly at Jose and Tommy. "You better leave now or they'll be carrying you out.' One of the sons said.

Both were leering at Tommy when Juan put a hand on Robert's gun. When Robert turned to him, Juan put his finger to his lips. "No need."

In an instant, both of the Sloane boys reached for their shoulders. They'd been shot and their faces turned white. One of the boys slumped to the floor and the other fell over on the table they were sitting at, crying out in pain. Their father's mouth was open and he turned toward Tommy Sanchez.  "Jack, the same thing will happen to you unless you put your gun on the table."

Jack was stunned. It seemed that he was trying to decide what to do but he complied. "Turn around Jack I'm putting handcuffs on you. You better talk to your boys so they don't try anything else."

Juan and Robert helped the two sons up and told them and their father to sit at the table. Tommy asked if there was a doctor or vet in town. The bartender said he could send someone for the vet. A half hour later the vet arrived. He checked the wounds on the two boys and said they were lucky. The bullets had gone through both shoulders. He stopped the bleeding and bandaged the shoulders. All this time the father and his two sons said nothing.

"It's too late to take these three to Santa Barbara today. Robert, can you and Jose put us up for the night. If not we can go to Franklin's place."

Robert smiled. "We have plenty of room and we'd be delighted to help you out. Those three horses are valuable and would be hard to replace, but what we saw today will stay with us forever.'

"Jose you and Robert take the horses home. Juan and I will follow you with the three prisoners. Do you have a place where we can lock them up tonight?"

We have a storage shed and Rene and Armand will watch them until you're ready to leave tomorrow morning."

After they tended to their horses and fed the three members of the Sloan family, they all sat down to a French Dinner prepared by Sophia, Robert's wife. Robert brought out a few bottles of White Bordeaux. Tommy learned of their time in New Mexico and he told them of his life as a Sioux Brave. Jose wanted to know how he learned to be so fast with a handgun. "I practiced a lot. That's the only thing I can attribute the gift to. I think I'm instinctive; I seem to be able to tell when they're going to reach for their guns. Do you worry that the Mexicans will bother you here?" He asked Robert.

How do you know about that?" Robert asked.

"Juan checked with Albuquerque to see who we were dealing with. I know you're French and I assumed you were part of Maximilian's cadre. This is America Robert. The Mexicans have no right here. If they come, most of us will stand with you; no longer are you alone."

"I appreciate your words. We've been looking out for ourselves for so long that we didn't know there were people like you we could count on."

"The Wellingtons told us about a confrontation between Rene, Armand and some Spanish youths. The Wellingtons didn't know you emigrated from Mexico and were part of Maximilian's cadre. Who do you think told the Spanish family about that?" Tommy asked.

"I have no idea."

'The Spanish family's name is Hernandez. We've never met them. Unless they have ties to the Mexican Government, someone told them to be on the lookout for French-speaking people. If you don't mind, I think I'll make some inquiries and see what I can find out." Juan said.

Tommy and Juan reached Rancho Del Prado around noon the next day and immediately sent for the doctor. After treating the wounds, the doctor cleared them to be taken to Santa Barbara. The vaqueros guarded the three that night at the ranch and in the morning Tommy sent four other vaqueros along with an arrest report with the three Sloanes. They were dropped at the jail. Jacob Thunder, wired Tommy at his ranch when they secured the three.

After the two long-time friends said goodbye to Tommy and Juan, they talked about the confrontation in the saloon.. "I heard about him, but I thought it was one of those things that grow larger the more times it's told. I'll be honest with you, I didn't see him draw." Robert said.

"I was standing beside him and wondering what he was going to do if they drew on him. It was obvious they were getting ready. It seems as though I blinked and they were reaching for their shoulders. They never touched their guns at all. I can't believe it happened. He was so cool about everything as though he knew what was coming. I still can't believe it. Rene and Armand listened to the story and asked his father to tell it again. "I don't believe it but I believe you." Rene told his father.

# CHAPTER 11

The Sanchez wine was well received by their friends and it was selling in many of the stores in Solvang, Santa Ynez and Santa Barbara. They had fifty acres in grapes and Tommy had approached several wholesalers in the Los Angeles area to see if there were interested in selling his wine. With fifty acres planted and producing, he had a glut on his hands and needed to move many of the barrels stored on the ranch. He found two wholesalers in Los Angeles and two in San Francisco that were interested. Tommy settled on one in each city.  Over the past year they moved nearly one hundred barrels of wine to Santa Barbara and then by ship to Los Angeles and San Francisco. He wanted to double the shipments.

The trip over the San Marcos Pass was tedious and took nearly a day. Tommy would send three vaqueros in his largest wagon once a month. Last month he met with his Los Angeles distributor at Rancho Del Prado and reached an agreement to double his shipments, while maintaining the one a month to San Francisco. He'd already purchased two more large wagons of comparable size and had sufficient number of barrels on hand to meet the new demand. He felt he could support the increase; if not, he had sufficient land to plant more in grapes.

The barrels he was using were coming from San Francisco, but he found a craftsman in Santa Ynez who could make them at his ranch; the overall cost would be significantly less. He set up a shop in the back of the large barn for the craftsman and two helpers. Two of the vaqueros were used part-time in the operation. Six months after he increased the number of shipments, a load of wine was hijacked, just after the vaqueros transporting the barrels, passed San Marcos Road on the Santa Barbara side of the pass. The vaqueros were roughed up and then hog-tied. They managed to get loose, and get a ride to the sheriff's office and report the theft.

Jacob Thunder, the sheriff, wired Tommy the details of the robbery and asked him to meet him where the robbery took place, the day after tomorrow. He made arrangements to house the three vaqueros until Tommy arrived.

Juan and Linda had come home last night after the sheriff contacted Tommy. The next morning, Tommy rode to his son's house near the trout pond on his property. He was just in time for lunch and Linda prepared the two men chicken salad sandwiches and Juan opened a bottle of his step-father's wine. While they sat outside overlooking the pond, Tommy told him about the robbery.

"I hope you can go with me to meet Jacob Thunder, see what he found out and what are my legal options?" Tommy asked.

"I have a client coming into the Santa Ynez office tomorrow. Let me go into the office today and see if one of my young lawyers is available to meet with my client. It's a small case and either one of my young associates can handle it. What time do you want to leave?"

"Let's leave at four in the morning and perhaps we can be back the same day. I'll have Tomas come and get you. We'll go down in a wagon, have breakfast at Kinevans and bring the vaqueros back and perhaps some of the wine if we find it."

They drove one of their large rigs and planned to meet the sheriff at noon; they were only ten minutes late. Sheriff Thunder, his deputy and the three vaqueros who were robbed met them, exchanged pleasantries and showed Tommy and Juan the exact spot of the robbery. "How many robbers were there?" Tommy asked

Each of the vaqueros said, "four."

Tommy continued questioning the driver. "Did you see their faces?"

"No. They were wearing masks."
"What about distinctive clothing or any scars?"

"They wore blue jeans and plaid shirts. There was one thing I remember. One of them had on spurs and those spurs were silver colored."

"Did they approach you on foot or by horseback?" Juan asked.

"They came from both sides of the road on foot and yelled stop or we'll shoot. We didn't see them as we approached the spot. They must have been hiding behind rocks or in dense grass. When I didn't stop, they fired two shots over our heads and I pulled up the horses and jumped down." The vaquero who was driving said.

"Tell us in your own words what you remember, after you were stopped." Tommy asked one of the three vaqueros.

The vaquero told them in Spanish what happened.. "After we stopped, the four came from either side of the road and lined the three of us on the side of the wagon. We all had our hands in the air and that's when they punched us in the stomach with their rifles. The three of us fell to the ground. They gagged us and tied our hands behind our back.."

"Did you see which way they went after they left you?" Juan asked.

"No. But we checked for tire tracks from the heavy wagon. They went directly toward Santa Barbara." Another vaqueros responded.

"How far did you track them?"

"To Calle Real and when they turned toward Goleta we lost their tracks. A farmer with a load of hay came by and we caught a ride to the sheriff's office." Another vaqueros responded to Tommy's question.

"What about the horses they rode here?" Tommy asked.

"They must have gone a different direction because we never found any of their tracks. I have a funny feeling that there was someone else with them and that's who moved the horses." One of the vaqueros responded.

Tommy was sure there was something else, so he continued questioning the vaqueros. "Was there anything else that was unusual or stood out to you?"

"One of the robbers called another Marshall." The driver said.

The sheriff responded to the dialog. "After we were told about the robbery we tried to find any tracks on Calle Real. We drew a blank. They must have hidden the tracks someway. I had my deputies ask some of the merchants on the way to Goleta to see if they saw the wagon with the barrels. No one saw anything. The wagons could be in a barn someplace in the area but no one is coming forward with any information. I notified the steamship company and the railroad to be on the lookout for the wine barrels."

They were still at the scene of the robbery when Juan asked the sheriff, "was the tree up there used as the staging place for the theft?" Juan pointed to a large oak that was about thirty feet from the robbery site on the north side of the road.

"To the best of our knowledge, they staged there." The grassy area has been trampled down by three or four horses.

"I believe they could see the wagon as it passed San Marcos Road. My question is how did they know you were coming that day and at that specific time?"

"You're right. How did they know?  My guess is that it wasn't random. They may have been tracking our shipments for some time. We'd been transporting our wine every month and generally near the end of the month and most probably on a Thursday. With the new contracts in Los Angeles and San Francisco we're transporting twice a month. It wouldn't be hard to put that information together, especially if they had someone working at our ranch or at one of our vendors who comes to the ranch on a scheduled basis."

"How big of a loss is it?" Thunder asked.

"Ten barrels is about three thousand dollars." Tommy smiled.

How many bottling companies are in the Santa Barbara area?" Juan asked Jacob Thunder.

"There's only two that I know of. It could be one of them and then again it may be a freelancer that wants to get in the business quickly"

"The barrels could be broken down into bottles and sold\under a different label. But it would be pretty hard to hide the horses and wagon. Maybe that's where we should concentrate initially and see if it bears fruit.. Thank's for coming down. I hope we have good news shortly. Thunder shook hands with everyone.

Tommy, Juan and the three vaqueros stopped at Kinevans on the way back to have something to eat. They drove home in twilight and arrived at the ranch after ten that evening. Linda and Sarah were waiting and the four had a couple of glasses of wine on the rear patio and talked about the robbery.

"Do you think it could be one of our vaqueros?" Sarah asked the two men.

"I'll talk to Tomas. Every one of the vaqueros has been with us some time, but the barrel maker I hired hasn't. He may be innocent, but that's where I think we'll start." Tommy sipped his wine as he was talking.

With the three vaqueros back at the ranch, everyone knew about the robbery. The first person Tommy and Juan talked to the next morning was their foreman, Tomas

Tommy asked Tomas if any of the vaqueros could be involved in the robbery. "I knew you would ask that question, so I thought about it a lot. I don't believe any of my men are involved.".

"What about the vendors who come here?"

"Most have been coming for many years. There are a few new ones but I know all the delivery men. Frankly patron, I think they'd be too afraid to steal from you. Your reputation is great in the area. Maybe someone is watching outside the property and put two and two together."

"What about the barrel maker? What do you think?"

"I don't know. He keeps to himself and does his work. Personally, I don't like him."

"Any particular reason?"

"He doesn't make eye contact with you when you're speaking to him."

"He and Juan went to the rear of the barn to talk to the barrel maker. His name was Henry

Wilcox. He smiled at Tommy and Juan as they approached him. "I guess you're here to talk about the robbery." Wilcox said.

Tommy noticed that he had his head down as he was talking to them. "Yes. Do you have any idea who robbed our shipment in Santa Barbara?"

"No, I don't."

"There's a possibility that someone either here at the ranch or perhaps a purveyor passed on our shipment date to the bandits. Have you seen anyone that was looking us over that seemed suspicious to you?"

"I'm sorry, Mr. Sanchez. I didn't see anyone that would be doing that."

# CHAPTER 12

One thing was certain in the marriage of Tommy and Sarah Sanchez and that was her annual shopping trip to Santa Barbara. Sarah looked forward to it; Tommy did not. They left around noon and stopped at the Arlington Hotel for their two night stay. Sarah wanted to have an early evening so they could be at the shops at ten the next morning. Tommy wanted to go out and have dinner on the beach. Sarah won the contest, they ate at the Arlington.

They dined on deep sea scallops and a bottle of Sauvignon Blanc. Sarah was excited and consumed three glasses of wine quickly. This was only her second trip from the ranch this year and the wine was making her a little tipsy. She kept flirting with Tommy mussing his hair, squeezing his hand and running her fingers up his thigh. He hadn't seen his wife like this in some time and he was flattered. He called for the check and escorted her to their room on the second floor. When they got off the lift, she danced all the way to their room.

When they enter their suite at the hotel, Sarah excused herself and went to change.

Tommy undressed, got into bed and dimmed the lights. Sarah came back into the bedroom completely nude. She danced around the bed and when Tommy reached out to grab her all he saw was someone who jumped on the bed and then quickly skipped off the other side. "Oh, you want to play do you?" Tommy smiled.

Sarah was elusive and she got behind one of the stuffed chairs and when Tommy reached out to her, he fell over the chair. "I thought you were nimble?" Sarah laughed out loud.

The chase was on and both knew the outcome. As Sarah tried to jump on the bed again, Tommy threw his arm around her waist and the two fell on the bed with Sarah on top. The inevitable happened and they made love for an hour and then fell asleep in each other's arms.

They ordered breakfast in their room and enjoyed a repeat performance of the previous evening. "I love you Tommy and today I'm going to spend a lot of our money. What do you think of that?"

"I can't wait. I hope they have comfortable chairs in the twenty or so stores we're going to. Money had been no problem for the Sanchez for many years. Tommy made his money in Mexico when he was in the cattle business and subsequently in San Diego in land development.

Sarah had an annual income from the oil leases she and her brother had on the property their family-owned. In addition, she was a well-known artist, and her paintings sold in the Santa Ynez Valley, Santa Barbara, and San Francisco. She and Tommy invested her funds for their children's future. Her assets took a hit years ago when she paid off her brother's debts he incurred going through a nasty divorce.

Their fifteen thousand acre ranch with cattle and wine income is what they lived on. Sarah had initially purchased five thousand acres and when they met, Tommy purchased an adjoining ten thousand acres

True to her word, Sarah did spend a lot of money which made the storekeepers happy and Tommy smile. They went back to Arlington and made plans to go south along the beach to one of their favorite restaurants for dinner, know as The Cave.

Their driver was on time and when Tommy told him the destination, he replied. "It's a good restaurant. You'll enjoy the cuisine and the wine."

There was a couple they knew from Santa Barbara that was finishing up as they entered. They spent a few minutes talking to them before they were seated at one of the prime tables against the wall. Tommy ordered a bottle of a Grenache. He smelled the cork and tasted the wine to see if it wasn't spoiled. "This is a pleasant wine but it has a familiar taste to it. Sarah, taste this wine and tell me what you think."

Sarah sampled the wine twice. "You're right, this is very familiar. If I didn't know better, I'd say this is our wine we're sampling."

Tommy asked the waiter to pour some more wine in his glass. He did another taste test. "This definitely is our wine. Waiter, please send for the manager."

They'd eaten in this establishment many times and were friendly with the manager. When the manager arrived, he asked, "is there a problem with the wine Mr. Sanchez?"

"Both my wife and I have tasted it and have come to the conclusion that this bottle of wine with the label, The Gold Vintage, came from my stock."

"The manager looked shocked. "This is impossible. We purchased three cases from the Gold Vintage Winery last week. Everyone who's tasted it loves it."

They should. As I said it came from our winery. Three weeks ago, a ten-barrel shipment of our wine was stolen right here in Santa Barbara near the San Marcos Pass. Tell me the name of the person or persons that sold you this wine?"

"Sir I can't do that. The seller is a well-known businessman in the city."

"I've already filed a claim with the sheriff, Jacob Thunder and I intend to sue to get my wine back. If you're a party to the theft, you'll need a good lawyer. Now you can give me the name now because we're going to the sheriff as soon as we leave here and swear out a warrant on this establishment. So it's your choice."

The manager seemed unsure what to do, but he also knew of the legend surrounding Tommy Sanchez and the last thing he wanted to do was antagonize this man. "His name is Gerald Henderson. He owns the Valuable Freight and

Livery Company on Lower State Street. This is probably just a misunderstanding."

"I think we'll pass on dinner this evening. I would advise you not to contact Mr. Henderson. You might have to explain your action to the sheriff. I'll take this bottle of wine with us as evidence."

"Their driver was surprised to see them leave the restaurant so early, but he quickly brought the carriage around to the entrance. "Are you feeling okay, he asked Tommy?'

"We're fine. Rather than go to the Arlington, we want to go to Sheriff Jacob Thunder's home in the San Roque District. Tommy gave him the address and directions.

When they arrived at the sheriff's residence, Tommy went to the front door while Sarah waited in the carriage with the driver. Jacob answered the bell and was surprised to see Tommy Sanchez standing on his porch. "What a pleasant surprise. Please come on in."

"My wife is in the carriage. If it's okay with you I'd like to have her join us. I'll have my driver wait. This shouldn't take too long."

Thunder's wife, Angel, was a petite Chumash woman who spoke mostly Chumash and some Spanish. Sarah was fluent in Spanish and while the men talked in Jacob's office the two women had coffee in the drawing room. Sarah and Angel had met while Jacob was campaigning for sheriff and were friendly. Tommy told Jacob what he found out and although he didn't suggest collusion between Henderson and the restaurant manager, Thunder saw it as a possibility. "I'll meet with both tomorrow morning and see what I can learn. If it's Henderson, he probably used his livery stable to store the wagon before they offloaded the wine and bottled it. You needn't do anything else. I'll take care of this and let you know what I found out."

They hadn't eaten dinner and it was still early so they went back to Arlington and had dinner in their beautiful dining room. "It's been an interesting day. We started it off in the right way, perhaps we could end it the same way." Sarah smiled.

"I'm ready when you are." Her husband responded.

# CHAPTER 13

As Tommy and Sarah were leaving the Arlington Hotel on their way home, Jacob Thunder called on Gerald Henderson at his livery stable on lower State Street. He was in his office going over some paperwork when the sheriff entered. "This is an unexpected pleasure to see you sheriff. Is this business or pleasure that brings you here so early?"

"It's a little of both. I haven't been here before, why don't you show me around and tell me about your business."

Henderson was surprised at the visit and wondered what the sheriff really wanted. "We no longer have horses at this location. All of them have been moved to our Goleta stable. Santa Barbara is growing and it wouldn't be prudent to have the smell of horses on Main Street. We load the wagons here and bring the horses when needed. Primarily, we use this location as a freight storage and delivery building. Even though it's fairly new, the lower part of state is changing and I'm thinking of demolishing the building and putting in retail shops. What d you think?"

"You've a keen eye for progress. I think you're onto something. I heard about a new association to clean up this area. Are you a member?"

"I'm one of the original members. I've been contacted by two retail companies that want to move in when we we're ready."

The sheriff looked at Henderson for a few moments and made the livery stable owner uncomfortable. "Would you like to go back to my office and tell me why you're really here, sheriff?"

When they were seated in the freight office, Thunder came to the point. "We had a robbery on the pass, near Foothill, several weeks ago; the thieves stole ten full barrels of wine off a delivery wagon.. They also roughed up the delivery personnel and left them tied up. We investigated but were unable to find the barrels, the wagon and horses or the thieves. The wine was valued at Three Thousand Dollars. The owner of the wine is a well known individual in the area. One might say, he's even a legend."

"What does this have to do with me sheriff?"

'This individual and his wife went to The Cave Restaurant last evening and ordered a bottle of wine. He sampled it; it tasted familiar. He asked his wife to taste the wine and she immediately said it came from their vineyard. The man asked the manager about the wine. He stated that he bought three cases from your representative. Their bottle of wine· came from those three cases."

"Well, I won't deny that we might have sold three cases to The Cave, but we purchased the wine from a distributor in town and bottled it ourselves at our bottling warehouse."

"Do you have the invoice for the purchase?"

"I do but it wouldn't do you any good, because we blend all our wine with some other wine and that's what we sold to The Cave. I'm sorry for the theft of this man's wine but he obviously knows nothing about wine. With the blending, he couldn't possibly tell that the wine came from his vineyard."

"He seemed very positive and he's been producing wine at the same location for fifteen years."

"What's the name of this man?"

"Tommy Sanchez of Santa Ynez"

Henderson was holding a cigar as he talked to the sheriff. At the mention of the name, he dropped ashes on his pants and had to move quickly to avoid being burned. As he brushed off the ashes, he blurted out, "the gunman?"

"I don't think he likes to be referred to as that, but I think we're talking about the same person."

Henderson recovered his composure and responded. "I stand by my statement. Any further discussion on this matter must be in the presence of my attorney."

"I must insist upon visiting your bottling plant and talking to your wine maker. If he confirms what you say, then I'll look elsewhere. I would like that visit to be today."

"We can leave now if that will satisfy you. I have nothing to hide. The sooner we can clear this up, the happier I will be." Henderson glared at the sheriff, showing his displeasure with this visit.

Thunder wasn't naïve, before he visited Henderson this morning, he sent his chief deputy to interview the manager of The Cave and pick up the remaining cases of the wine in question. He didn't want the manager nor Henderson to have time to come up with an agreed to explanation. The deputy returned with the wine and said that the manager of the restaurant was very cooperative.

Thunder's impression of Henderson was that he was shifty and it would be difficult to get enough evidence to arrest him and any others working for him. Sanchez was a good friend and one who supported him in his run for his office. Jacob was going to do everything he could to find the ones responsible for the theft.

It took them forty five minutes to reach Henderson's bottling plant. Stacked against the walls were cases of wines, all bearing the Golden Vintage label. The wine maker was on duty and was working on a blend of wine in the lab. Henderson introduced the two men and allowed the sheriff to ask him questions

"Where does your wine come from?"

"We purchase wine from many growers in the area. Perhaps there are six growers who are our primary sources."

"Ten barrels of wine were stolen near San Marcos Road a few weeks ago. Could some of that wine have reached you?"

"It's possible. I have three barrels that we purchased from a new company last week. I believe we saved two of the barrels. They're outside against the rear wall."

The three men walked outside and examined the two barrels. The sheriff asked the winemaker if he could see the bottom side of the barrels. Two husky workers tipped the barrels on their side. Both clearly bore the Rancho Del Prado mark on the bottom."

"Sheriff, I didn't know anything about this. I swear." Henderson was pale.

The sheriff looked at the winemaker. "Do you have an invoice for the barrels?"

"I do but I don't know if it will help you. I don't recognize the name on the invoice. Two guys showed up and said they had extra premium wine available and would I be interested. I sampled the wine and thought I was getting a premium wine at a good price. It was so good that I had it bottled without blending it."

"Did you sell any of that wine to The Cave Restaurant?"

"I believe we did."

"I want the remaining two barrels and any bottles from those barrels that you didn't sell. I'll give you a receipt. If what you say is true, your company won't be prosecuted." Thunder told Henderson.

Sheriff, I swear to you that I didn't know about this. I'm not a winemaker. I took my man's word that we blend everything here. What are you going to tell Sanchez? He's not someone that I want as an enemy."

"Unless something else shows up, I believe you're in the clear on the robbery and subsequent scam. I'll make sure Tommy Sanchez knows that you cooperated fully." Thunder shook Henderson's hand and left. He could tell that Henderson breathed a sigh of relief.

The **Sanchez Family** always threw a large party the Saturday before Christmas.  It was primarily to celebrate the holidays but also to acknowledge all those who helped Rancho Del Prado during the year. Annually, they added more names to their invitation list. Eventually, they realized something had to give. This year Tommy and Sarah reluctantly set the limit at seventy-five. People came from as far away as Los Angeles and looked forward to the event.. Plush tents were set up with several blankets over straw for a bed with privies outside for those who couldn't make it home that evening. The guests didn't view the tents as an inconvenience but more as an adventure. In many cases, the tents became an extension of the party and lasted well into the morning.

Others had friends or relatives in the area who they could stay with. Franklin and Maria Sutter and their children would stay with her brother Enrique, at his estate in Buellton, while the newest members on the list, the St.Pierres and Santanas would stay in the two guest rooms at Rancho Del Prado. The exception was the three boys, Rene, Armand, and Fernando who bunked with the vaqueros while Jose's daughter and James Jefferson of the Pinkerton Agency would stay with Juan and Linda Sanchez at their home near the pond in the south part of Ranch Del Prado. Jacob Thunder and his wife were guests of Silas and Marjorie Smith.

James Jefferson had been a close friend of the Sanchez Family for nearly fifteen years. It was Sarah who he met first. It was during the time when she was the destitute widow of Crazy Horse, the Indian Hero of the Battle of the Little Big Horn. She was living on a military outpost barely surviving, teaching the children at the fort, while raising two teenage children and being considered an outcast by the wives at the Army post. Her sin was that she married an Indian who helped annihilate the famous Seventh Cavalry and their leader George Armstrong Custer. To make matters worse, her daughter had taken up with an Indian Brave and was living on a reservation.. What gave her more grief was her son, Juan, who was the leader of eight to ten teenage renegades getting involved in petty thefts, horse stealing and just being malcontents.

Juan ran away several times and Sarah was beyond hope when she met Jefferson, who was an agent with the Pinkerton Detective Agency. He found her son and returned him to her at the fort. But Juan ran off again mainly because the soldiers harassed him and called him Indian Trash, It wasn't until she met Tommy Sanchez that Juan became the son she always wanted. Tommy was introduced to Jefferson and through Jefferson's contacts, they learned where Juan and his gang were hiding out. The two took a train to Missouri and found Juan and his gang at a saloon in the southwestern part of the state.

A confrontation ensued and Tommy and Jefferson disarmed the gang. It was the speed of Tommy's draw of his revolver that impressed Juan more. Tommy talked to Juan as though he was his brother and told him that his renegade days had to end. He'd either start obeying the law and go home to his mother or he was looking at the gallows.

Juan was in awe of Tommy, but most of all, it was the restraint he used in subduing Juan's gang that he most admired. He agreed to take a chance and go home. It wasn't only the fancy shooting that won Juan over to Tommy; it was the hope for a future that Tommy gave him. Both were half-breeds and could see themselves in the other. Tommy eventually adopted the young man, with Juan's and his mother's approval. Today Juan is a prominent attorney with a beautiful wife who is expecting.

By noon of the next day most of the guests in the tents had departed; though some went fishing at the pond on the south part of the property and left the following day. Others visited the mission, four miles away or the adjacent town of Solvang. The three boys that stayed with the vaqueros got up early, tended to the animals and helped cleanup. That's when they learned about the theft of the wine barrels in Santa Barbara.

After breakfast, they shared this information with their parents. Immediately, Robert and Jose asked if they could help. Tommy indicated that the sheriff was investigating the matter, but he didn't know what the status was. When Thunder and his wife came by to thank the Sanchez' for the superb party, Jose and Robert asked if they could talk to Jacob privately.

Robert was the first to speak. "Our families want to thank you for sending Tommy Sanchez to help with the theft on our property. We know you cover a lot of territory with very few deputies. I wonder if you'd be interested in appointing my friend Jose, to be one of your deputies for the Los Alamos and Santa Ynez area. Jose was the sheriff in Albuquerque New Mexico for ten years and the people kept electing him after each term ran out. If you're interested, you can contact the town and ask them what his capability is."

"In addition, we'd like to help with your investigation of Tommy's stolen wine barrels. Robert's son Rene is twenty-three years old and quite handy with a gun. He's never been in trouble and is very competent. I'd like you to give us a chance to prove our capability. With Rene's help, we could check into the barrel theft. What have you got to lose? You don't have to pay us initially. We owe it to Tommy and this will give you a chance to determine if we fit in with your law enforcement plans." Jose said.

"You caught me by surprise. I don't have an answer today. It's true that we're short-handed and need someone in Los Alamos that could come to Santa Ynez or Santa Maria, but I can't make that decision. It's up to the Board of Supervisors to authorize the position and then fund it. Give me a couple of weeks to check you out and if Albuquerque says you re good, then I'll talk to the Board of Supervisors.

The sheriff knew he was shorthanded, so the first thing he did when he returned to Santa Barbara was wire the town of Albuquerque New Mexico to inquire about Jose Santana. Three days later a telegram from the mayor said, "if you can hire him, don't waste any time. Do it."

The board of supervisors wasn't that quick, but Thunder was persuasive and they granted his request for funding for a deputy in Los Alamos for three days a week. The sheriff wired Franklin Sutter, who was Santana's neighbor, and told him it was good news and for Santana to come to Santa Barbara at his earliest convenience and be sworn in.

Three days later Jose Santana and Rene St. Pierre arrived at the sheriff office. Both were sworn in as deputies. "Jose, your position only allows you to work three days a week. If you're on a case and need more time, go ahead and finish it but I'll have to get approval to pay you for the extra time.  Okay/' Jose nodded his concurrence.

"Rene, I have temporary authorization to bring in a deputy as needed. I'll be able to fund you for three days and that's all. If we need more time, we'll play it by ear. And like Jose, you need to finish the task and then hope I can get you paid. Do you understand?  Rene nodded his acceptance.

Thunder took out a city map of Santa Barbara and Goleta. "Here's where the robbery took place and here's where they tracked the wagon." Thunder put an X on the map for both places. He showed them where Henderson's freight office, livery stable and bottling plant were located, It was Henderson's Bottling Plant where his wine maker bottled some of Tommy's wine sold to The Cave..

The last place he showed them was The Cave Restaurant. He explained about the three cases of wine that were bought by Henderson.s wine maker and how it ended up at the Cave Restaurant. The owner of The Cave is a man by the name of Staley. He may not be involved.

"Do you think Henderson is involved?" Rene asked

"I don't. I think the winemaker saw an opportunity to get some premium wine at a low price and didn't think beyond that." The sheriff responded.

"We should keep our contacts to a minimum while you're in town. Someone may be watching who comes and goes at the sheriff's office. Use the phone whenever possible."

The two started to leave but Thunder wasn't finished. "I have another suggestion; look at the tax rolls. Henderson may own other properties that were used in this theft. I may not think he's involved, but I've been wrong before. I'm relying on you for a thorough job. And don't forget about the owner and the manager of The Cave Restaurant. He may have been just trying to get premium wine at a low price. Then again he might be involved. Finally, how did the thieves know when and where to strike? My guess is there's someone in Santa Ynez that may have tipped off the robbers."

The two new deputies rode down to the wharf, had lunch, and discussed their options. "I think we ought to take the sheriff's advice and look at the tax rolls first. If anything catches our attention we can look at the plat book and see where the property is located." Jose said.

They spent nearly three hours going over the tax rolls and found three properties that were owned by Gerald Henderson, two of which were in Goleta. Owen Staley, the owner of the Cave Restaurant, owned four other properties in Goleta. However, William DeWire, the manager of the Cave wasn't listed on the tax roll. They couldn't think of anyone else that could be involved at this time.

It was getting late as the two left the county clerk's office. With the addresses from the tax rolls matched against the city and county street maps, all that was needed was to view the properties in the daylight and go from there. Although their joint farm was at a break-even stage, the money they'd get as deputies would help in purchasing items, such as fertilizer and supplements for the horses. A hotel wasn't in their budget. They'd brought their sleeping bags and decided to go to the scene of the robbery and camp out there.

After making a cursory look at the place, they set up their blankets on the grass the bandits used as a staging place. They wanted to get an early start in the morning, but as soon as it was light, they carefully inspected the area and found two cigarette butts and a discarded bag that held tobacco. The brand was Old Hickory.

Other than an occasional coyote singing to them, they had a peaceful night, ate bacon and potatoes that Sophia prepared for them and made their way to Goleta. The first two properties they visited were vacant lots owned by Gerald Henderson. The four properties owned by Owen Staley were more interesting. One housed a small bottling company. They were denied access to the building by the workmen there, even though they showed their badges. "Come back when you have a warrant." That's what the foreman said to Jose.

Another of Staley's properties had a vacant warehouse on it. They looked in all the windows of the warehouse and concluded that there was nothing suspicious inside. A third property they visited had a barn on it that was locked. Rene went around the back of the barn to see if he could see what was inside, but there were no windows. They did find a crack in one of the vertical boards and Rene could make out two wagons inside. "What do you think? Rene asked Jose.

"Maybe it's a coincidence but it appears that Owen Staley has potentially all the pieces of the puzzle we're trying to solve. He has wagons under lock and key, he has a bottling plant we can't visit and the wine was found in his restaurant. I know we started out looking at Henderson as the thief but maybe it's Staley. We have no evidence and I'm reluctant to have the sheriff get a warrant to open the warehouse where the wagons are. It could turn out that neither of the wagons are Tommy's." Jose said.

"We've got to do something. The barn has a door on the second floor which was probably used to toss down hay. Maybe with a little help I can climb up there and get in." Rene smiled.

"What if we're caught?"

"We'll show them our badges and see if we can get them to open it for us."

Rene stood on his horse and reached the bottom sill. Jose handed him a stick and he was able to pry the door open. Rene pulled himself up and entered the second floor. It was only a matter of time before he made his way below and checked the two wagons. When he stayed over with the vaqueros during the Christmas Party, they showed him a unique thing about Tommy's wagons. A metal star was stamped into the bottom of one of the floor boards under the driver's seat.

Rene crawled under the first wagon but it was dark. He struck a match and found the metal star; he didn't bother checking the second wagon. Rene retraced his steps and swung down into his saddle. With Jose's help they closed the second-floor door. The two made their way to the fourth property owned by Staley, but it was a vacant lot and none of the mules were there. They called the sheriff who was still in his office. Rather than meet there, they selected a small saloon on lower State Street. "I can be there in a half hour." The sheriff told the two men.

Jose and Rene got to the saloon fifteen minutes ahead of the sheriff. It gave Jose time to finish writing his report  When Jacob Thunder arrived, Jose and Rene told him what they found. "Let's go see Judge Wharton. I think he'll sign a warrant. Give me a few minutes to write one up and we can go to his office."

With a warrant in hand, the three rode out to the barn owned by Staley. The sheriff cut the lock and Rene opened the door. There was only one wagon left inside. Rene checked and it wasn't Tommy Sanchez' "Someone must have seen us go inside and then moved the wagon. Why don't I follow the tracks and see where it went?" Rene left Jose and the sheriff, got on his horse and slowly tracked the wagon wheels. He found the wagon in a vacant field about a mile away.

When he returned, Jose and the sheriff said they wanted to check the sales yard in Goleta to see if Tommy's mules were there or had been there; it was on the way to the vacant lot. The sales manager allowed them access to all of the corrals. There were no mules there, but the manager's records showed that there were four mules sold last week to Greystone Farms. "Who sold them to the Sales Yard?" The sheriff asked..

"Some guy walked in with the four mules and we bought them. It happens sometimes and we don't get a name. I didn't know they were stolen."

As they left the Sales Yard, Jose asked the sheriff if he thought they had enough evidence to arrest Staley.

"I don't think so. There was a wagon in his barn that belonged to Tommy and then someone moved it. Staley would probably say that you made a mistake. But while we're out this way, let's check Staley's bottling warehouse and see if any of Tommy's barrels might be there? You said they wouldn't let you in"

As they approached the warehouse, workers were loading barrels of wine onto a wagon. "Look's like we're here just in time. Jose, you and Rene round up everyone and bring them outside while I inspect the barrels."

There were seven people inside the warehouse. One tried to run for it but Rene was too quick and too powerful. He overwhelmed the man immediately. Jose had them sit outside with their backs against the front wall of the building. Several barrels were in a corner of the warehouse. Rene and Jose tipped them on the side, while the sheriff looked underneath. "These are Tommy's barrels. They still have his initials on the bottom of the barrel." Thunder told the other two.

They took everyone into custody and read them their rights. Rene and one of the workers rode over to the vacant lot and brought back Tommy's wagon. They had the workers load Tommy's barrels in the wagon and then drive it to the jail. When they arrived at the jail, the sheriff had the wagon with Tommy's wine barrels put behind the building and he locked up the seven he arrested at Staley's Bottling Plant.

Thunder sent two deputies with an arrest warrant for Owen Staley. The owner of the Cave Restaurant was at home having a nap. He was charged with grand theft and brought to the jail. He was livid and yelled at the sheriff. "When my attorney gets done with you Thunder, you'll end up on some form of welfare, because I'll sue you for everything you have."

The sheriff wired Tommy Sanchez that they found his wagon and some of the barrels, but not the mules. The sheriff asked him if he could come to Santa Barbara in the next few days.

# CHAPTER 14

Tommy and three vaqueros drove to Santa Barbara at the end of the week and met with Jacob Thunder in Goleta. They brought along four horses that were wagon broke. The sto0len wagon was in storage along with four cases of wine and seven barrels of his wine "Do we know what happened to the mules and the other barrels of wine?" Tommy asked the sheriff.

"No. My best guess is they bottled the wine and sold it. We interrogated all the workers at Staley's Bottling Plant, but they're not talking. We know the mules were sold at the Sales Yard. Mr. Staley has been non-committal since we arrested him He and all his workers are out on bail. Jose and Rene found a used bag of tobacco and two cigarette butts at the staging site near San Marcos Road. One of Staley's men smokes that brand. The Prosecutor is charging that individual with assault on your vaqueros. I don't know if it'll stick, but maybe he'll turn on someone."

"Is it possible that I could meet with Staley and ask him to return our wine?"

The sheriff smiled. "I can't do that Tommy. We have to follow procedures. We plan to have the trial next week. My assumption is that he'll be found guilty and go to prison."

Tommy and the three vaqueros returned home without the wine which was being held as evidence until the trial. Jose and Rene travelled with them.

Since the investigation into the theft of ten barrels of wine started when Tommy Sanchez and his wife tasted their wine at the Cave Restaurant, owned by Owen Staley, Tommy and Sarah would be called as witnesses at Staley's trial. It was expected to last two days and the Sanchez' would be called the first day. They left home with Jose and Rene, three vaqueros and a large wagon the day before the trial began and were in court at the designated time.

The prosecutor was very thorough in outlining the case against Staley and his first two witnesses, Jose Santana and Rene St. Pierre, acting Santa Barbara County Deputies, told the court about finding the wagon and barrels of wine. Their testimony alone was sufficient to establish that Owen Staley was behind the armed robbery of the wine. The workman who used the brand of tobacco found at the robbery staging site was questioned thoroughly but wouldn't admit to the assault on Tommy's vaqueros.

When it was time for Tommy and Sarah to be called as witnesses, the prosecutor took his time and kept his questions very simple. However on cross examination, the defense attorney was not as considerate. He tried to brow beat Tommy and when that failed to stir Tommy, he started to raise the issue of his use of a weapon. "Mr. Sanchez, you're known for your prowess with a handgun. How many men have you killed?"

The prosecutor was out of his seat immediately and yelled, "Objection."

The judge knew Tommy quite well and was aware that the defense might try to cloud the issue by painting Tommy as the bad guy and not Staley. "Objection sustained. Keep your questions relevant to the theft of the wine. Mr. Sanchez's history is not relevant to the robbery that is the subject of this trial."

The defense attorney realized the judge wouldn't allow this line of questioning, so he concentrated on Tommy's ability to pick out his wine in a blind taste test.

Juan sensed what tactics the defense would use at the trial and he spent a half day with Tommy and Sarah going over their testimony and insuring that they could pick out their own wine. "Okay Mr. Sanchez, I have a bottle of Grenache that you tasted at the Cave Restaurant several weeks ago. "I'm going to have you do a blind test to see if you really can pick out your own wine." The defense attorney said.

The prosecutor knew this was a red herring. "I object, your honor. The taste test is unnecessary. Mr. Sanchez wine was found in Mr. Staley's Bottling Plant and in his restaurant. In addition, we have two witnesses who saw the Sanchez' wagon in Mr. Staley warehouse along with barrels of the Sanchez wine at the same place. That should be sufficient to establish the crime."

"I'm going to allow the taste test, but I want to be sure that we're using Mr. Sanchez wine. The sheriff has cases of the wine in question. Three of those bottles came from the Cave Restaurant the day after Mr. and Mrs. Sanchez were there. I want that wine used in the taste test."

They recessed the court for thirty minutes while the sheriff gathered the wine for the testing. They conducted two blind taste tests and in both cases Tommy picked out his wine. Sarah was asked to do one blind taste test and she picked out their wine. The trial was over the next morning and the jury retired to decide on the verdict.

However, while the jury was deliberating, Tommy and Sarah were asked to meet with the prosecutor and defense attorney. When the four were seated around a conference table in the courthouse, the defense attorney spoke. "We have an offer for you, Mr. and Mrs. Sanchez. If you accept the offer, we'll take it to the judge. Mr. Staley will plead guilty to all charges, apologize for the inconvenience, and reimburse you for your loss of wine, time, and mules in the amount of six thousand dollars. In addition, Mr. Staley will accept probation, do some community service, and pay a fine of One Thousand Dollars. All the workers arrested by the sheriff will be set free. They were acting under Mr. Staley's orders."

Tommy looked at the prosecutor and asked his opinion. He responded. "I think it satisfies my office. "

"I want ten thousand dollars for my wife and I. In addition, I want two thousand for expenses and five hundred dollars each for my three vaqueros who were assaulted. We were put through a lot of aggravation and I won't accept a penny less. In addition, I want the name of the individual who either works at my ranch or comes to the ranch enough so he knows our routine and passed it on to Staley or his representative."

"Sir I have the authority to accept your offer." The defense attorney said.

The signed offer was presented to the judge by both attorneys and accepted by his honor. The jury was dismissed, but when polled by the reporters outside the court, they divulged that it was unanimous for guilty.

One hour later a draft of twelve thousand dollars was turned over to Tommy and Sarah and five hundred dollars in cash for each of the three vaqueros. Staley named the recently hired barrel carpenter as the source of the time and schedule of the shipment. Tommy saw his barrel carpenter in court the first day. It was possible the man would beat them back to the ranch and wouldn't be seen again.. Owen Staley and his men were set free.

Over lunch at the Arlington, Juan asked Tommy and Sarah if they were satisfied with the settlement. "I think there's only one thing missing, but I don't think the settlement was entirely unreasonable. There's a big storm coming in tomorrow. I think Sarah and I need to head home. We may have to stop at the Kinevans if the storm catches us on the way back."

They said goodbye to Juan, thanked him and off they went to the valley. They were accompanied by the three, vaqueros who were driving the wagon. In the back were seven barrel's of wine and four cases of the same wine returned by the sheriff. In addition, Jose and Rene travelled in the back of their carriage. The storm hadn't reached the pass, so they stopped long enough at the Kinevans to get something to drink and have a nice steak before heading home. Tommy presented the cash to each of the three vaqueros who were assaulted by Staley's men. They were so grateful, that they wanted to pay for dinner. They made it home before thunder and lightning flashed across the sky.

It was too late for the train to Los Alamos, so Jose and Rene stayed over in the guest rooms. Before heading home, they borrowed a rig from the ranch and visited the Wellington sisters and set up a date two weeks hence.

In Santa Barbara, the storm hit about six in the evening and electricity in the town was non existent. The wind howled and the waves crashed down upon the pier. Light poles were down and many of the trees along the beach were uprooted. Owen Staley was at home with his mistress. They had an early dinner and drank a bottle of Tommy Sanchez' wine. They decided to make it an early evening and retire to bed. Before they retired, Staley's mistress asked him if he was satisfied with the outcome of the trial.

"It looks as though they had me dead to rights and I didn't want to go to jail. I'll get back at Sanchez another day for the hard bargain he drove."

It was about two AM when someone dressed entirely in black, climbed up to the second floor of Staley's mansion. He opened one of the sliders to the master bedroom and made his way to the bed where two adults were sound asleep. The woman was lying on her back as the black clad stranger put a hand over her mouth and showed his knife. He taped her mouth, rolled her on her stomach, bound her hands and put a mask over her eyes.

When Staley woke, he tried to rise but the black clad figure put a knife to his throat and told him to be quiet. The intruder tied Staley hands to the bed post, his feet to end of the bed and put tape over his mouth. He held a shaving mug and a straight razor, which he sharpened in front of Staley.

With one quick move he sliced off Staley's left ear lob. The restaurant owner tried to cry out but any noise was muffled by the tape on his mouth. Tears came to his eyes and his face grimaced. "If you try to rob anyone else in the area, I'll come back and cut off your other ear lob."

The black clad figure went out the slider and slid down the rope he left tied to the balcony; he disappeared into the night.

The deputy on duty at the sheriff's office was called to Owen Staley's house at four in the morning. Staley face was a mess, his bed sheets were covered with blood and he was in a rage. "Tommy Sanchez was here and cut off my ear lobe."

"Senor Staley, you said the intruder was wearing a mask. How can you be sure it was Senor Sanchez?"

"He's done this before. The former editor of the Santa Barbara Register was mutilated by him. I want him arrested."

"By this time the sheriff arrived and had to listen to the hysteria from Staley. The deputy had the situation in hand so Jacob Thunder went to his office and wired Tommy Sanchez at home. He asked if he'd been home last evening. Tommy sensed there was a reason the sheriff asked the question, so he woke Jose and asked him to respond.

Two days later Staley's attorney visited the sheriff and asked if Tommy Sanchez was under arrest. "There were two deputies with Tommy Sanchez and his wife the night of the assault; all four were in Santa Ynez at the time. We'll investigate the break-in at Mr. Staley home, but it wasn't Tommy Sanchez."

Owen Staley stayed close to home the next two weeks but the word got out that someone had cut off his ear lobe. When Staley and his mistress were seen at another restaurant in town, he couldn't help but hear the snickers from the other patrons. Soon the couple couldn't go anywhere in Santa Barbara without feeling scorned.

The day after the trial, the barrel carpenter didn't show up for work. Tommy sent one of the vaqueros to his home in Santa Ynez to see if he was sick. The vaquero reported back that the house had been cleaned out and one of the neighbors indicated the tenant moved north.

Within six months, Staley decided to sell his holdings and move to San Diego. Juan and Linda Sanchez bought the Cave Restaurant and immediately purchased several barrels of wine from his mother and step father.

# CHAPTER 15

Because of its large Hispanic population, the City of Santa Barbara decided to celebrate Cinco De Maio on an annual basis. They invited the Consul Generale, the Honorable Gustav Lopez, a former Army General in The Army of Benito Juarez to be the honorary chairman of the event. He had an office in Los Angeles. Tommy and Sarah Sanchez had been going to this event the past five years. They decided to attend this year and invited The St. Pierre's and Santana's to be their guests

Other than the Christmas party at Tommy and Sarah's place and the party at the Sutter's Ranch, the two families hadn't been out in public. They weren't afraid of being seen, but the events of the past few years made them cautious. The families talked it over and decided they'd been in hiding long enough and wanted to go. Tommy invited them to spend a night at Rancho Del Prado and be his guest at the Arlington the following night. Fifteen of them went in three carriages the next day to Santa Barbara. After an early breakfast, they set up chairs on State Street at eight AM and found a good spot to watch the parade, which was to start at ten in the morning.

The food and liquid vendors were up and down the street selling to the willing patrons. Tommy Junior and Helga nearly got sick on the number of chorizos they ate. The parade lasted thirty minutes and the Guest of Honor rode in the first carriage. Robert and Jose saw him and recognized him immediately, but didn't believe he saw them. Riding in the back of the carriage with the Consul Generale and his wife, were Mr. and Mrs. Hernandez from Santa Ynez. It wasn't lost on Tommy who the couple was and what it meant to Robert and Jose and their families.

After the parade, they went to Oak Park where most of the festivities were held. By four in the afternoon, everyone was tired, so they got in their carriages and went home. Their guests stayed overnight and left early the next morning, grabbed the train to Los Alamos and were home in the afternoon. They were happy they went.

Over the past five years, the two families increased their herd of horses, broke the wild ones and sold them to the neighbors. Without the Comanches providing them a steady source of animals, they had to seek other ways to increase their livestock. There were many rustlers in the area, but they avoided them at any cost. Armand and Fernando found some mustangs in the hills west of Los Alamos. They captured about two dozen and brought them back to their farm.

Jose broke most of the mustangs, but they weren't as easy as the ones the Comanche's sold them. The net result was it took longer to bring them to market and the demand wasn't as great. Money was always an issue with the two families because their reserves weren't as high as they were in New Mexico. Fernando and Armand worked at Franklin Sutter Ranch, while Rene, Jose and Robert did most of work at their farm. Occasionally, Jose and sometimes Rene would earn money as deputies.

They hadn't experienced any more theft after Tommy Sanchez caught the three Sloanes and arrested them. Currently the three were serving seven year terms in Colorado. Maria was coming of age and one or two of the young men in the area were calling on her.

The mayor of Santa Barbara and Tommy were hunting friends and two days after the parade in Santa Barbara, the Mayor asked Tommy if he'd host the Consul Generale at Rancho Del Prado. Tommy agreed and Sarah and Naomi prepared the guest rooms and a celebratory dinner to include some of their friends in the valley. Two days later an entourage of two carriages came down the main entryway to the ranch, led by six dragoons. Tommy and Sarah saw them come and waited on the porch to welcome them to their home.

In addition to the Consul Generale and the mayor, Silas and Marjorie Smith, Enrique Contreras and Linda and Juan Sanchez were invited. .Because the Consul Generale and his wife had to return to Santa Barbara early the next morning, dinner of steak, mashed potatoes, salad and apple pie was served at four thirty at the main table in the dining room. Tommy provided the wine and the toasts were many, lasting into the early evening. Silas and his wife went home, but Enrique Contreras spent the evening at Juan's and Linda's home.

A point of contention came shortly after dinner was over. The Captain of the Dragoon asked to speak with Tommy Sanchez. "Sir we're here to guard the Consul Generale during his stay. Your foreman Tomas said that we couldn't position guards around the hacienda at night."

"He's correct. This Ranch is guarded at night by my vaqueros on shifts throughout the night. I can't have another armed group attempting to do the same thing. I don't want to take a chance that one group mistakes the other for an intruder. In fact there'll be no weapons inside the hacienda other than mine."

"Senor, I have my orders and I must insist that I be allowed to carry them out."

"Wait here Captain Suarez. I'll be right back." Tommy went back to the dining room and asked the Consul Generale to join him in the main hallway.

The two men met with the dragoon captain and he told the Consul General what the problem was. Tommy explained the procedure he used at the ranch and why he couldn't have two different armed groups outside at the same time.

The consul thought for a few minutes and proposed a solution. "Perhaps the captain and his men can patrol the area until midnight and your men can have the midnight to daylight shift. There would be no conflict then." He smiled at Tommy.

"Mr. Consul Generale, I respect your position but you and your men are guests at our ranch and as such you're under my protection. Your men will not have weapons outside at night nor in my house. If that is not acceptable, then I will call the hotel in Santa Ynez to see if they have accommodations for you."

"Senor Sanchez, that won't be necessary. While we're here, we'll operate under your rules."

The consul turned to his dragoon captain, "Captain, you and your men will adhere to the policies of this ranch. The captain saluted and made his way to the bunkhouse.

The next morning after a light breakfast everyone complemented Sarah Sanchez and her husband for a wonderful evening. The Mayor and the Consul Generale left for Santa Barbara around ten. Enrique and Tommy made plans to fish at the south pond in the afternoon; Juan was to join them. Tomas saddled Tommy's horse and boxed up his favorite fishing rod: Linda had agreed to feed the men lunch; Tommy brought three bottles of wine.

As usual, Enrique caught the first fish and gloated over the other two. He had the honor of opening the first bottle of wine. "I had an interesting conversation with the Consul Generale last evening. Perhaps because we're both of Hispanic descent, he asked me some interesting questions. He asked if there were any French Nationals living in the area."

"I told him there were none that I knew of though I'm acquainted with Robert St. Pierre. I thought it was an unusual question, so I asked him why he was interested. He said that some of Maximilian's staff, who were of French descent had escaped, killed some soldiers while escaping and made off with substantial gold from Mexico's reserves."

"He's talking about Robert St. Pierre and Jose Santana, isn't he?" Juan asked.

"Why would they suspect that some of Maximilian's cadre would come here? I don't like it. Someone had to tell them about Robert and Jose and I think I know who did. Armand and Rene were on a picnic with the Wellington sisters when the two Hernandez boys started an altercation and made some unflattering remarks about their French Heritage. I saw Mother and Father Hernandez riding with the Consul General at the Cinco de Mayo Celebration in Santa Barbara." Tommy told the other two.

"I know they came from New Mexico, but I didn't know why they left. Jacob Thunder hired Jose Santana and Rene St. Pierre as deputies because Albuquerque gave Jose a strong recommendation. Let's hope the Mexican Government isn't planning on sending some of their people here to check on Robert and perhaps Jose." Juan said as Tommy opened another bottle of wine.

"Do you want me to make some inquiries?" Juan asked Tommy.

"I don't know how much credibility we should give to the questions posed by the Consul Generale. However, I think you should see what you can find out in New Mexico and see what relevance it has to the inquiry."

# CHAPTER 16

Juan had previously dealt with a legal firm in Santa Fe and felt comfortable enough with their senior partner to ask about Jose Santana and Robert St. Pierre of Albuquerque. What he got from the law firm was perhaps more than he bargained for. It was a summary of the court case brought by Jose Santana, the Sheriff of Albuquerque. The document was complete and Juan took several days to read and reread the transcript.

Luckily, Juan had some business with Mrs. Cota in Los Alamos and set aside a half day to talk to his step-father about the New Mexico Case. They met in Tommy's office at the ranch and enjoyed a glass of wine while they discussed the subject of Jose Santana and Robert St. Pierre.

"So there was some meat to the inquiries by the Consul Generale.?' Tommy asked.

"It looks that way. The Mexican Government sent two groups to Albuquerque to bring back St. Pierre and Santana. The first group of three arrived and never returned to their country. The second group of fifteen had three survivors, who Santana arrested and charged with attempted murder. The Mexican Government got involved as did our State Department and an agreement was made between the two countries. The three Mexicans were released and the Government of Mexico agreed never to pursue Robert and Santana for taking gold or killing Mexican Troops. At no time did Santana or St.Pierre confess to theft or for killing the Mexican Soldiers in Mexico at the check points."

"It seems that the Mexicans are contemplating reneging on the agreement. What about the gold?"

"Whether there was ever any gold stolen is mute. Jose Santana stated at the trial that the only money they had when they left Mexico was given to them by his father, a well-known attorney in Mexico City. Additionally, Robert St. Pierre testified that Maximilian gave him three thousand Pesos as they were escaping. The court of New Mexico concluded that there never was any gold taken from the Mexican Government."

"What about the killing of soldiers as Jose and Robert were escaping?"

"That's probable. Six Mexican Soldiers were killed defending a checkpoint in Northern

Mexico and four more at another place.. It's also a fact that two of Jose's and Robert's bodyguards were killed at one of the checkpoint. But this is also mute. The agreement was that Mexico would not pursue the two families." Juan took another sip of wine and when Sarah entered the office with crackers and cheese, he helped himself to a handful.

"You always have a good feeling for these situations. Do you think the Mexican Government plans a raid up here to bring back Santana and St. Pierre?" Juan asked.

"Oh, I think that's an absolute. My best guess is they'll come by boat and strike inland. When they'll do it is the real question. I've got to think about this and I don't know how much time we have."

If there was anyone who had an understanding of the politics in Mexico, it was his old friend Carlos Quintana. Tommy hadn't seen his friend in years, though they corresponded on a semi-annual basis. Carlos was the brother of the woman that Tommy was to marry. She was killed while Tommy and she were enjoying a picnic near her home. Five men came upon them as they slept on a blanket near a small pool. They shot Tommy four times and gang raped his intended.

When the father found them; he cried.. His daughter was dead and the son-in-law to be was near death; his betrothed's family didn't think he'd live. He willed himself back to good health and pursued the killers. Eventually, he captured all the men responsible for her death and turned them over to her father to mete out justice.

Subsequently, Carlos and Tommy were business partners in land speculation in San Diego, where they made a lot of money. Carlos also saved Tommy life, when a former law enforcement officer tried to assassinate Tommy.

Carlos' father had passed away, but Tommy was still close to the family. He decided to write his friend and ask his advice. Ten days later, Carlos responded and indicated he had business in Los Angeles the following month. He asked if it would be convenient to visit with Tommy at his home during that time. The answer was swift with an invitation to visit and stay as long as he wanted.

Tommy asked Silas Smith if he'd like to visit Jose and Robert. He told him what his concerns were and what he intended to do. They took the train in the morning and had their horses placed in a special car. He'd checked with Juan and received Mrs. Cota's permission to travel on the western part of her land grant. What

Tommy wanted to see was what type of shore line she had with the ocean. They spent the afternoon riding along the beach looking up at the plateau above. It was mostly sheer cliffs but several areas had eroded and it would be easy to offload troops and small mechanized weapons, to climb up the bank and reach the top of the cliffs. They'd telegraphed Franklin and his wife of their intent to be in the area and asked for lodging for two days. They wanted to talk to both Franklin and the two families bordering his property.

The Sutters went the extra step and invited the two families for dinner to meet with Tommy and Silas. The three boys and Maria were there as well. After the table was cleared, everyone grabbed something to drink and they listened to Tommy explain why he was here. He told them about the conversation the Consul Generale had with Enrique Contreras. "Robert and Jose, you may think I overstepped my bounds, but I'm concerned when any outside group decides to come into our valley with their own agenda."

"At my direction, Juan contacted a law firm in the state of New Mexico and we received a transcript of the trial you were involved in with the Mexican Government."

"You could have come to us. We would have been honest with you." Robert responded.

"To be honest, I wouldn't know what to ask had I not asked Juan to investigate. If what I think is going to happen, I would've been remiss and put my friends the Sutters at risk as well as Mrs. Cota."

"I didn't mean it the way it sounded." Robert said.

"Silas and I, with Mrs. Cota's permission, rode the western perimeter of her land. If the Mexicans send anyone to capture you, they'll probably come by sea, offload at Mrs. Cota's property and attack you from the west."

"You seem to think that it's a foregone conclusion. They promised at trial that they would leave us alone."

"I think they lied."

"We appreciate your interest, but why have you interjected yourself into this situation?"

"The Consul Generale made his inquiry at my ranch. I didn't appreciate that. I also didn't appreciate him brining armed soldiers to our place. It was as though he was sending us a message. My friends and I don't like to see people taken advantage of, It isn't the first time all of us have gotten together to repel those who sought to harm us. If you need further corroboration, just ask Franklin and Silas. I think they feel the same as I."

"We had a handle on the situation in New Mexico. But here, it's a different game. They could be on us before we even knew it. In the other two cases, they sent three soldiers and when that didn't succeed, they sent fifteen. What's to prevent them from sending fifty? We wouldn't stand much of a chance." Jose said.

"To answer your question, Silas, Franklin and I could raise fifty men in a moment's notice if we had to. And then there's Mrs. Cota and Enrique Contreras. We can be a formidable force. I think we should take this opportunity to strengthen your defenses and especially develop an early warning system. I can send some of my vaqueros to your place for a couple of days. They could be very helpful."

"I can provide five or six of my men for a few days if that would help." Franklin said.

Tommy and Silas were invited by Robert to stay at their place their last night. Both men accepted and spent one full day surveying the access to the five hundred acre farm. When they left, Jose and Robert felt more comfortable. Tommy also shared with them that his friend from Mexico would be visiting next month and Tommy would have him meet the two families.

"With the name of Sanchez, aren't you half Mexican?" Rene asked.

"Actually, I'm half white and half Sioux. I didn't have an American name until I was about sixteen. I picked the name Sanchez because I looked Hispanic."

Carlos Quintana came one afternoon with his wife Felicia. Tommy was in the barn working with Tomas training a new colt they bred last year. The two men hadn't seen each other since San Diego. Tommy couldn't make the wedding of his friend. because he was chasing down Mr. Brown who'd kidnapped Sarah.

Carlos' wife Felicia was of Mexican descent and was equally as beautiful as Sarah Sanchez. The two women admired each other immediately. Over the next two days they recounted old times and Tommy told Carlos about the Consul Generale and what he thought was going to happen. He gave Carlos a copy of the transcript of the trial between the Mexican Government and Robert St. Pierre and Jose Santana.in Albuquerque, New Mexico. Carlos asked if he could spend the rest of the afternoon reading the document.

Tommy allowed Carlos to use his office while he and Sarah took Felicia for a ride around the ranch with special emphasis on the pond. Juan was in Santa Ynez at one of his offices but Linda was home and gave the visitor a tour of her home.

Juan and Linda joined the two couples for dinner and after dinner the three men discussed the trial and the Consul Generale. This was the first time that Carlos had met Tommy's step-son. When Carlos learned that Juan was a prominent attorney, he wanted his opinion on the situation.

My step-father has a better feel for what's going to happen than I do. If he's correct, the Mexicans are in for a shock. The US Government got involved in New Mexico. Here the situation will be different. The people here don't want to be invaded by anyone and they'll go to greater length than New Mexico in protecting the two families but also prosecuting any Mexican Soldiers who survive, The authorities in this county will ask for the death penalty. They won't let the federal government get involved and they'll use force to rule their territory. The Mexican Government can't use our State Department to bail any survivors out this time."

Carlos was sober. "You paint a stark picture of the situation."

"If the Mexican Government sends troops, they'll be fought by ranchers and their men, who'll be defending their country. Tommy and his four close friends can field fifty men at a moment's notice. Robert and Jose were by themselves in New Mexico. Here they'll be a minority in the group that fights. That's as candid as I can be."

"Would you be part of the group?"

"Where my father goes, I go."

"What about the soldiers who were killed in Mexico by the two men?"

"I don't fault them for protecting themselves and their family but there should be some sort of compensation for those who lost their lives."

"I know President Diaz quite well. He's trying to be a good leader but like the rest of us, he has blind spots and wants an eye for an eye, even though his government signed off on the New Mexico agreement. When I return, I'll talk to him about the situation and what he's up against. You promised that we'd go fishing. What do you say?"

The three got up and asked the women to join them tomorrow; they said no. "To be honest with you, we haven't had enough time getting acquainted," Sarah said.

The men left early the next morning. Naomi fixed them breakfast and lunches to go. The women were still in bed; they'd been in the living room having sherry when the three men went to bed.

The women got up soon after the men left. Sarah was curious about a comment Felicia made to Carlos yesterday. "Who is Maria Conchita?" Sarah asked Felicia as the three women were having lunch at the nook in Sarah's kitchen.

"Maria Conchita was Carlos' sister; she was killed many years ago. She and I grew up together."

"Is there something more that I should know?"

"I don't want to say anymore. It's a sad story. It would be best if your husband told you."

"You mean Tommy knew her."

"She was his betrothed."

# CHAPTER 17

One of the things they wanted to do before Carlos went back home was for the two of them to meet with the St. Pierres and Santanas. They took the train to Los Alamos along with two of Tommy's horses and went through Franklin's property to get to the two-family farm. They stopped and talked to Franklin for a half hour before they continued on.

It was Robert who met them as they came into the front yard; Jose was out in the barn. They had a foal last night and he was making sure the young colt was nursing correctly. Robert invited everyone into the main house and Carlos was introduced to everyone in the family. Angelica served lunch of Enchiladas and Refried Beans. Tommy brought three bottles of Red Wine and they had a leisurely lunch with a lot of conversation.

Both Robert and Jose told Carlos their stories including their escape from Mexico and the two raids they repelled in New Mexico. "Tell me about the Mexican Soldiers who were killed by you?" Carlos asked.

"At one check point, the guard became suspicious and raised his gun to fire on us. I shot two of the soldiers, Robert and our bodyguards shot the others and we lost two of our party. We were on the run and suspected that Juarez would try to stop us. We didn't have time to bury the dead. At another checkpoint, we were cleared through, but one of soldiers became suspicious, told us to stop as we were leaving and it was them or us. I'm a soldier; I was trained what to do in these type of situations. I have no regrets." Jose said.

"What about in New Mexico?"

"They sent three men and we saw them in town and became suspicious and watched them come to our farm and look us over. Subsequently, they checked out of the hotel in town and we followed them. When we caught up to them, we gave them a chance to surrender. They chose another option and we killed all three. In the second case, we knew they'd come back and we prepared for them. Fifteen came in with guns firing. There was no attempt to capture us; they meant to kill us. We killed twelve of them and captured the other three. One of our people wanted to kill them but Jose was the sheriff and wanted to follow the law. I agreed and he arrested the three, charged them and they were brought to trial. The rest is in the court transcript." Robert said.

"What about the gold?"

"There never was any gold. The only money we had was from my father plus Max gave us a few Pesos as we were escaping. The rest we earned." Jose responded.

"Someone knew you were here, who do you think notified the Mexican Government?"

"We have no idea. The boys had a run in with two Spanish speaking young men, named Hernandez, but that was the only confrontation anyone in the family had." Robert told Carlos.

Both of our wives are European; all our children were born in the United States. Yet, the Mexicans were indiscriminate when they came after us. They fired on all of us. If it was only Robert and me they were after, why did they try to kill all of us?" Jose was red in the face as he talked.

"I'm not a member of the Mexican Government. I'm a businessman who supports the current government and who knows the president. When I return, I will talk to him about the situation and why he should not send anyone to bring you back or worse. But, that is all I can do. Tommy and I are like brothers. If you have doubts about me, ask him."

The train went through Los Alamos going north early each morning and south in the late afternoon. Carlos and Tommy picked up the train for home at four PM, loading their horses and finishing off the last of the wine they brought with them. "Are you satisfied with their story?" Tommy asked.

"It seems plausible. The thing that would give me pause if I was in the Mexican Government is the number of soldiers they killed while escaping. There's a fine line between what's prosecutable and what's not. I'd like to know if the Mexican Government has arrest warrants on St. Pierre and Santana."

"What are you going to do?" Tommy asked.

"I'll talk to Diaz who's the President now and see why he still wants to pursue the two. The big question is, what are you going to do?"

"If they come again, they'll have me to deal with. I don't like it that they came two times and agreed to let them go. If it's me making the decision, whoever comes is not returning."

Carlos and Felicia left for Los Angeles in the morning. Tommy had two of the vaqueros take them to the train station in Santa Barbara. Their plan was to finish up some business in Los Angeles and then vacation in San Diego for a week before returning home.

He and Tommy had been developers in San Diego and Carlos still maintained a residence there overlooking the ocean in a seaside community known as Loma Linda. At least once a year they travelled to this bustling city just over the border. In the future, they would spend a week here and another in Santa Ynez visiting Tommy and Sarah.

When Carlos and his wife arrived in San Diego, he had reservations about spending a week here. "Felicia, I must return to Mexico City and talk to President Diaz. Mexico is my country and I feel he is making a mistake if he sends troops to bring back the two who served on Maximilian's staff."

"You mean Jose and Robert. I don't think they can harm our president."

"It's my friend Tommy that he should fear. Tommy knows that Diaz is going to send troops to bring back Robert and Jose and I know he's laying a trap."

"Is Tommy that powerful?"

"He's the most powerful individual I know. It was superhuman what he did in bringing back those men who killed Maria Conchita. Rather than kill them, he gave them to my father. He literally carried me for three days when I was mauled by a mountain lion. When he sets his mind to a task, he's insurmountable. Diaz should not send any troops. It's a death sentence for them."

They took the train the next day to Mexico City and two days later Carlos had an audience with Diaz. The president and his father were good friends. Carlos met the man many times when he came to their hacienda. He graciously welcomed Carlos and asked him why he was here.

After listening to Carlos for thirty minutes, he frowned. "It's too late. The troops are already on their way. I can't recall them. Why do you think we won't prevail? Is it because of this man Sanchez?"

Mr. President, you remember the story my father told you about the man who went after my sister's killers?"

"I remember. He didn't kill them but brought them to your father to mete out the punishment. The man felt that Don Francisco had first claim. What a man. I hope to meet him someday."

"That man is Tommy Sanchez. He has said those who come, will not return."

"How close are you to this man?"
"He's the best friend I ever had."

"It is what it is Carlos. I must have your word that you will not communicate with this man until this is over. I vowed that the two would stand trial in Mexico City."

"Sir, I will not violate your trust but I must caution you that this will be a disaster for us. Please do everything you can to recall the soldiers."

A week after the Quinteros left, Sarah approached Tommy with a question. "What was Maria Conchita Quintero to you?"

The room became so quiet that you could hear a pin drop. Sarah was worried that she raised a subject that was off-limits. "I guess I always planned to tell you some day but I could never find the right time. Now is as good a time as any to tell you."

"The first member of the Quintero family I met was Francisco. We subsequently went into the cattle business together. I was a successful businessman when I was introduced to him, but under his tutelage, I became very successful. He was more like a father to me than a friend. His son Carlos was close to my age and we became instant friends. As our friendship grew, we became business partners and developed a significant part of San Diego and made a lot of money."

"Before the San Diego venture, we went hunting and Carlos was mauled by a mountain lion. I brought him back home and he spent some time in the hospital recovering. The father was worried Carlos would die, so he sent for his daughter, Maria Conchita, who was away at school. Maria was ten years my junior but we fell in love and with her father's approval, planned to marry."

"Her father gave a huge party to announce our engagement. Early in the afternoon, we broke away and went to an oasis about two miles from the rancho and had a few glasses of wine and talked about our plans for a honeymoon. The day was warm and soon we fell asleep. I was awakened by a lot of laughter. Five men were tearing off Maria's clothes and when I started to rise they shot me four to five times in the chest and stomach and left me for dead."

"Don't tell me anything else. It has to be too painful."

"I think it's best that you know everything, especially what came later." Sarah started to cry and sat down in an overstuffed chair across from Tommy. She wondered if she opened Pandora's Box.

"After a few hours, Francisco became worried and went looking for us. He found me lying on a blanket surrounded by blood and Maria lying dead in the bushes. She'd been violated many times. The father and his help nursed me back to health; it took over three months. In the interim, Francisco called upon the authorities to find the killers. No one found anything of the five and the Mexican Authorities let the case die. In my view, they didn't want to go the extra mile."

"Didn't you worry that you weren't back to normal and wouldn't be able to find the killers?"

"Not for a second. I willed myself healthy and went after them. I wasn't part of law enforcement, so I wasn't constrained by the law. If I thought someone was lying, I would keep after them until they told me the truth. I stopped in a cantina about one hundred miles south of Francisco's Rancho. I had a hunch the killers came this way. I asked the bartender if he knew anything about the men. When he said he didn't know anything. I shot off his left earlobe. When he still didn't tell me anything, I shot off his right ear lobe. He told me some things and another patron told me the rest. It was he who led me to their hideout."

"I captured the five and brought them back and gave them to Francisco. For weeks afterward, I could hear their screams at night, but I did nothing and didn't want to know anything. I'm sorry if this story gives you pause."

"I'm glad you told me and I don't have any problem with what you did. I'm happy it was me you married because I know that if anyone hurts me or the children, you'll be unmerciful until you resolve the issue. How about lunch and a glass of wine?" Tommy smiled.

# CHAPTER 18

They arrived late in the afternoon and anchored off the coast directly across from Mrs. Cota's property. Aboard were twenty battle-hardened soldiers, led by Captain Rodriquez. The schooner, which embarked from Vera Cruz, was named Maria. Their commander knew he was taking a chance that they could be noticed, but he waited until six the next morning before he offloaded his soldiers. They came ashore in two-row boats with a total of fourteen soldiers. Captain Fernando Rodriquez left two soldiers to guard the row boats. Six would remain onboard to be used in an emergency.

The soldiers heading to the beach were heavily armed and carried minimal food and water. Their plan was to attack the farm, capture Robert St. Pierre and Jose Santana, make their way back to the boat and return to Mexico. They'd been briefed on the location of the farm, where to offload their men and how to scale the cliffs surrounding the Cota property. The vaqueros who rode for Mrs. Cota were up early and saw the soldiers doing a quick step across her property and realized they were Mexican Soldiers.

Four vaqueros, though unarmed rode up to the soldiers and demanded they get off the property. The Mexican Soldiers opened fire on the vaqueros and two fell to the ground wounded. The other riders for Mrs. Cota, picked up the wounded, rode back to the hacienda and told the foreman, Miguel Garcia, what happened. There were a total of ten vaqueros riding for the Cota Estate. Garcia wired Franklin Sutter, the sheriff, Tommy Sanchez and Enrique Contreras about the incursion. He told his riders to arm and wait for instructions. When he got the message, Franklin sent a rider to alert Jose and Robert at their farm. The Mexican Soldiers continued on.

Robert St. Pierre had supervised the upgrade of an early warning system, which consisted of a series of cans and strips of metal that would give off a sound whenever their fences were penetrated. He heard the sounds of the metal about the same time as the rider from the Sutter's arrived. He aroused everyone, passed out guns and ammunition and ordered everyone to defend the stations they drilled at for the past two weeks. The Mexican Soldiers took their time as they approached the large house where all of the inhabitants lived. Robert and the others fired from reinforced walls inside the house once the intruders were in range.

The Mexicans were patient. They divided up into four groups and used their fire power to see where the house was most vulnerable. The intensity of their firepower had its impact on the residents inside the house, especially the rear portion. But it didn't appear that the Mexicans were making any advance because of the fire being returned from the main house. After two hours of firing at the house, a definite hole appeared in the rear wall. Three Mexicans used axes to expand the breach and break into the rear of the building.

Robert, Jose and Rene rushed to repel the Mexicans who entered one of the back bedrooms, where Jose's daughter, Maria was.. Robert and his sons fought back and killed two of the intruders but the third grabbed Jose's daughter by the hair and pulled her toward the opening in the rear wall. "He's got Maria. Don't let him get away with her." Robert yelled.

Rene dove for the Mexican's legs but the young soldier was too quick and sidestepped Rene and pushed the girl all the way through the wall where she fell to the ground. Jose rushed to his daughter's defense but he and Rene collided trying to get through the opening at the same time and both fell to the floor. By the time they got up and went through the hole, the Mexican and Maria were with the other soldiers, who were setting up in a defensive strategy as they started to retreat to the shore.

The Mexican Soldiers used Maria as a shield. As Robert, Jose and Rene tried to follow, three of the intruders fired at them and they had to duck back inside the house. When they tried again, the Mexicans were in full retreat dragging Maria with them. The men at the farm couldn't fire because they might hit the young woman, so they followed at a distance looking for a moment when they could rescue her.

By this time four of Franklin Sutter's men arrived at the farm and began firing on the Mexicans, who were heading toward the beach. Mrs. Cota's vaqueros were now armed and were trying to cut off the Mexican's escape route. But the Mexicans were a well disciplined unit and they strategically used their captive as a shield and continued their move, though slow, toward the schooner. Two hours later Captain Rodriquez could see the cliffs in the distance and knew they'd get away.

Tommy Sanchez received the message from the Cota Rancho and he roused six of his vaqueros. They moved quickly as a cohesive unit gathering ammunition and saddling their horses.

Sarah and Naomi hastily got some food together and off they went. The sheriff wired the Los Olivos train station and ordered the train be held for Tommy Sanchez and his party. Tommy and his men boarded the train to Los Alamos and put their horses in a special car on the train

Tommy received one last wire from Franklin at the railroad station, indicating that Jose, Robert and their families were under intense fire and Franklin didn't know how long they could hold out. He hesitated before leaving because their last passenger hadn't arrived yet. Tommy didn't know how long he could wait and was ready for the train to start. Five minutes later Enrique and four of his men arrived and put their horses on the train. After Tommy and his group arrived in Los Alamos and unloaded their horses, they raced to the Cota ranch stopping only long enough to water their horses. One of Mrs. Cota's vaqueros was waiting and he led Tommy and his vaqueros to the cliffs overlooking the schooner at anchor. Enrique and his men went to the farm to help the two families, just as the Mexicans were retreating with Maria in tow.

Tommy took out his binoculars and looked down from the cliffs. He could see two soldiers guarding the row boats and he decided on a plan of action. Four of his vaqueros would go further north along the cliff and head down to the beach so they'd be coming at the men guarding the boats from the north. Tommy and the other two vaqueros would go along the cliffs further south and find a path to the beach. They would attack from both directions. The two guards at the row boats had no shelter other than the boats, but It still took an hour before they were subdued. Both were wounded in the melee.

Tommy and his group had control of any access to the schooner which was one hundred yards off shore. While they were involved with the two soldiers on the shore, the six soldiers who were on the ship climbed down into a row boat and started toward their two wounded compatriots. Two of Tommy's vaqueros shot at them as they boarded the rowboat. Two Mexican Soldiers were hit immediately and fell into the water; it was assumed they were dead. The other four turned back to the schooner.

In the interim, as the Mexicans with their prisoner moved toward the cliffs, Mrs. Cota's vaqueros were firing at them from the north side while Enrique and his men were firing from the south. Enrique didn't know the Mexicans had captured Maria until he saw her being used as a shield. He cautioned his men and only shot at the soldiers who would come open. Robert and his group were close to the Mexicans as they retreated but he wouldn't fire for fear he'd hit Maria. Rene finally made his way to the Cota group and told them to hold their fire.

Tommy regrouped his men and retraced their steps, climbing back up the cliff. After they tied their horses to some brush about a hundred yards away, they found defensible positions on either side of the path where the Mexicans came up the cliff. They knew it wouldn't be long now for the Mexicans to arrive. As the firing got closer, they got ready to attack. Tommy made one last check of his men. There were four north of the access point down the cliff and he and the other two were south of the same point. Each had a strong defensive position; each was an excellent shot with a rifle and each had been tested before.

As Captain Rodriquez and his men retreated to the access point to the ocean, There was only random firing from Mrs. Cota's vaqueros, Franklin Sutter's men and Jose, Robert and their sons. Tommy didn't know about the kidnap, so he ordered two rounds fired at the Mexicans. Soon, there was a white flag and Rodriquez approached Tommy and his men. He spoke in Spanish.

"Senor, we have a hostage. She's Captain Santana's daughter, Maria. We intend to take her with us to the schooner. If you value her life, let us by. If not she'll be shot and that will be on your head."

Spanish was really Tommy's second language and he had no problem understanding the Mexican captain. "You must understand that you won't be allowed to pass. There is only two ways this incursion by you will end. You will either die or surrender. We understand that the girl could be harmed but it will have no effect on my intent. Either surrender or die. It's your choice."

"Senor, I can't believe what you're saying. You mean to sacrifice a young woman rather than let us go?"

"We won't sacrifice the girl. You will. If she dies, I will personally kill you and all your men. You have very little time to make up your mind. I'll give you fifteen minutes to talk it over with your men. No matter what, you're not leaving this area. You either die or surrender."

The men including Robert and Jose closed in on the Mexican soldiers retreating with Maria to a point they were within firing distance.

Five minutes later Captain Rodriquez and his men were on the move toward Tommy and his men. Tomas and another vaquero with Tommy were the best shots with a rifle. Tommy ordered them to take out two of the Mexicans. Two Mexicans were hit in the head and fell over dead. Soon thereafter, the white flag went up again. When Rodriquez approached Tommy he was told to stop ten feet away. "Captain, give the order to surrender or I'll kill you where you stand." Tommy said.

"I'm under a white flag senor. Do you have no honor?" Rodriquez shouted for everyone to hear.

"You're the one who invaded our country and took a defenseless young woman. Either give the order or die. I'll count to ten. One, two."

"All right I'll surrender. I hope we meet again." Rodriquez gave the order to his men to drop their weapons and his men complied.

"If we meet again, the result will be the same."

The vaqueros rushed up to the intruders and made sure they weren't armed. Maria was freed and walked toward Tommy, who hugged her. By this time, Mrs. Cota's vaqueros arrived as did Enrique and his men plus Robert, Jose and Angelica, the girl's mother. The father and mother embraced their daughter and held her tightly.

Captain Santana thanked the Mexican captain for surrendering rather than causing more bloodshed. "On the contrary senor, we had no choice. That man said he wouldn't let us escape even if the girl was shot." He pointed at Tommy Sanchez.

Angelica heard the discussion between her husband and the Mexican Captain and walked over to Tommy. "Were you going to kill them all if they didn't surrender?" She asked.

"Angelica, if we allowed them to take Maria to Mexico, you may never have seen her again. The Mexicans would've had leverage over both families. Next, they would've demanded Robert and Jose. They weren't going to kill your daughter as long as they were here. I couldn't let them go."

By this time Jose Santana joined Tommy and Angelica. "I overheard what was said. Tommy got your daughter back. We couldn't let them take her. If I was in charge, I would've done the same thing."

"Maybe I overreacted Tommy. I know you wouldn't do anything to hurt Maria." Angelica said

The foreman for Mrs. Cota told Tommy that two of his vaqueros had died from their wounds. Jose walked his wife back to their daughter and helped them onto horses that Walter brought. Robert escorted them home. Jose arrested the surviving Mexicans. With their hands tied behind their back, he and Rene marched them back to Franklin Sutter's House. By wire, Franklin Sutter contacted the sheriff in Santa Barbara and through a series of messages summarized what had transpired.

Six of the twenty Mexicans had been killed, two by Robert and Rene, the rest by Tommy's Vaqueros. The two at the rowboats were wounded and attended to by Tommy's vaqueros. The schooner set sail and made its way south with four soldiers alive and two dead. They were subsequently intercepted by an American Frigate and everyone was taken into custody

It took four days to get all the prisoners to the Santa Barbara Jail. But it was as though the

Mexican Government saw the outcome as a possibility and their consul representative was at the lockup when the prisoners arrived. He demanded the release of the prisoners to him as the representative of the Mexican Government in America. He also wanted the ship returned to Santa Barbara, so all including the wounded could sail to Mexico.

Sheriff Jacob Thunder wouldn't be intimidated and he refused the demands of the consul. In fact, he wouldn't allow any visitors to see the prisoners. However, he did turn over the dead bodies to the consul. The wounded were being attended at the Santa Barbara Hospital.

# CHAPTER 19

The county prosecutor charged the remaining Mexican Soldiers with murder, attempted murder, conspiracy to commit murder and kidnapping. Each of the charges was a state crime. They weren't charged with invasion which was a federal charge. Two of Mrs. Cota's vaqueros were killed, Maria Santana was kidnapped and two of Franklin Sutter's men were wounded. The county supervisors were angry that America was invaded and even angrier that some of its citizens were victimized.

If the residents of the county weren't aroused at the arrest of the Mexican Soldiers, the Santa Barbara Register's Editorial Page further inflamed the populace. The writer encouraged the county to ignore the Federal Government and go for the death penalty. For a week, the writer continued his direct prose. There were daily crowds in front of the jail yelling death to the invaders. Sheriff Jacob Thunder was concerned and brought in a few retired deputies to help control and disperse the crowds. He asked Jose and Rene if they could come down for a week and help out

The problem was who was going to try the case, The County prosecutor didn't have the experience to handle a major case and he knew it. He met with the supervisors and recommended several quality attorneys but one of the supervisors from a northern district threw out Juan's name. There was no one more surprised than Juan Sanchez when the supervisors asked if he was interested. He told them in writing that he was flattered and he'd give them an answer in four days.

This wasn't the first time that Juan had jumped to the other side. He'd been appointed as Prosecuting Attorney in another case and had been successful. Before he accepted the appointment, he talked it over with his step-father, Tommy Sanchez. "Forget the honor of being asked. Can you emotionally press for the death penalty?" Tommy asked.

"I talked it over with Linda and feel the county is going to be under extreme pressure to let the soldiers go back to Mexico. I don't want that to happen. There is no question that I have reservations about the death penalty, but in this case where a foreign country invaded and several of our citizens were killed, I can live with it. I haven't agreed to take the case but if I do, I'll pursue it diligently.

"I've already heard from the US Secretary of State. He made sure I knew that the Federal Government wanted the Mexicans turned over to them. Anyone who takes this on is facing the might of the US Government. I think I'm up to it. You've taught me a lot but the most important thing you taught me is to be my own man. For that I thank you and I love you."

In addition to the Mexican Government Representatives and their high priced law firm out of Los Angeles, the Federal Government sent two attorneys and six Federal Agents to be sure that the Mexicans were protected. They wanted to supplement the county sheriff's department with two of their men. Jacob Thunder said "no thank you", and ushered the two out of his office. The secondary objective of the US Government officials was to intimidate Juan Sanchez The two federal attorneys, John Sturges and William Hines, thoroughly researched Juan's background. Their consensus was that when push came to shove, they could have their way with the half breed Sioux.

If Juan was surprised by his government's attitude, he could have fallen over when he found out that the Mexican Government claimed the Mexican weren't their soldiers but Volunteers. They claimed that the group was formed by ex-soldiers whose relatives were killed by Jose and Robert, though it would be difficult to prove that they were killed by the two men. The Mexican Government's position was that Robert St. Pierre and Jose Santana had committed crimes against the people of Mexico and the incursion by the Mexican Volunteers was to seek justice for their dead relatives.

Juan would learn from the consul representative that there were some men in the Volunteers whose relatives were supposedly killed by Jose and Robert, but they were a minority. The Mexican Representative further stated, "since the volunteers weren't part of the Albuquerque Agreement, it has no bearing on their action. The part where Robert and Jose were given amnesty and the Mexican Government promised they would never attempt to kidnap them had nothing to do with the Volunteers, who were honoring their relatives.

"There's no way to tell who killed the border guards." Juan countered.

"That's irrelevant. The Volunteers are convinced it was those two men and we, the Mexican Government, share their pain."

Within two days of that conversation, four more attorneys, arrived. Two were from Mexico City and two from Washington D.C. They presented their credentials to the County Attorney and said they would represent the Mexican Volunteers. They wanted to meet with their clients. Jacob thunder had no choice but to comply. The two from Mexico City were bilingual and the two from the nation's capitol were well versed in international law. Juan knew he needed some help and he reached out to James Jefferson of the Pinkerton Agency in Los Angeles.

The American Government was angry at the Mexicans for reneging on the agreement reached in Albuquerque, and for the subterfuge of the Volunteers. Still, they didn't want the Mexicans found guilty and sentenced to death. Santa Barbara County wanted the Mexican survivors hung. When the newspapers ran the article stating that the Mexicans claimed these were relatives of slain soldiers, there were many letters to the editor, still supporting the death penalty. Worse than that, the number of groups that came by the jailhouse shouting obscenities at the jailed Mexicans increased.

Sturges was obviously the lead Federal Agent and he asked for a meeting with Juan at his earliest convenience. Juan gave him several options and Sturges accepted a two PM meeting three days hence. Juan asked his stepfather if he wanted to be present at the meeting. Tommy Sanchez smiled.

The federal agent, arrived on time with two state department agents, though he hadn't mentioned bringing anyone with him, Juan smiled at Tommy as introductions were made. Sturges turned to Tommy. "What's your interest in this meeting?"

Juan immediately responded. "All questions will be directed to me, if you don't mind."

"Okay, why is a civilian part of our discussion today?"

Sturges asked.

"Mr. Sanchez was head of the team that captured the Mexicans and one of the most respected men in this area."

"It's the State Department that has the lead in this country on any matters involving another nation. We want you to turn the prisoners over to the US Federal Government. I assure you that we'll exact the highest penalty our country allows."

"We'll, we're not turning the defendants over to you. The Mexican Government claims they aren't soldiers but Volunteers, who are kin of the border guards killed. They will be prosecuted on the state charges of murder, kidnapping and attempted murder, whoever they are."

"Really, Mr. Sanchez, the Mexicans were defending themselves when the two vaqueros were killed. As far as kidnapping, they released Maria Santana unharmed. I don't think a court will convict the Mexicans on those charges."

"The vaqueros that intercepted the Mexican troops were unarmed and weren't provocative. They asked the invaders to leave their property. Some defense on the part of the Mexicans, don't you think? As far as Maria Santana, the Mexicans used her as shield to assist them in their retreat. If it wasn't for Mr. Sanchez, they'd be in Mexico with Maria. They had no choice but to release her."

All of a sudden, something dawned on John Sturges and he turned to Tommy.. "You have the same name as the county prosecuting attorney. Are you related?'

Juan smiled. Mr. Sanchez is my step father."

"I didn't know that you were going to have someone, not of the legal profession, attend this meeting."

"Really, who are these two men with you and what is their purpose here today?"

"Both are federal marshals and its common practice for me to have them with me when I'm out of town."

"When you asked for this meeting, I don't remember you telling me that you were bringing other people with you. Did I miss some correspondence you sent?"

"No. You're correct. I should have notified you who I was bringing. If you're amenable, I'd like to see if you will turn the case over to the federal government."

"I have the transcript on my desk of the trial in Albuquerque. I know you've read it. But just to be sure, I'll summarize the outcome. New Mexico turned the Mexicans over to our federal government who negotiated with Mexico. The Mexicans were set free in return for the Mexican's government's agreement, in writing, that they would never attempt another incursion into our country to kidnap Jose Santana and Robert St. Pierre."

"Now if you think this county is going to follow the New Mexico Plan, you've been smoking loco weed."

"The Mexican Government has assured us that they aren't their soldiers. They are volunteers who are seeking justice for their dead relatives. We can file in Federal Court to have the case tried there"

"Sure you can, but you still have to overcome the fact that we're not trying the Mexicans for Federal Crimes, but state only. The crimes the Mexicans are charged with are murder, attempted murder and kidnapping. If they persist that they are Volunteers, then this is not a country to country case."

"You know you can't win this contest between the state and the federal government. You're wasting your time."

"The county has spoken and I'm representing the county of Santa Barbara."

When the federal representatives left his office, Tommy asked Juan. "Do you think you can prevail? There's going to be tremendous pressure from them throughout the trial."

"All I can do if work with the cards I've been dealt. The two incursions into New Mexico and the Mexican's Settlement Agreement are points they can't hide from. I wonder how long the Mexicans will stand behind this gimmick of Volunteers. They looked like soldiers to you, didn't they?"

"They were soldiers. Rodriquez, their commander is regular army."

"The only thing I'm concerned about is whether our federal government will prevail and take over the case." Juan responded.

"I know you're busy but there's another issue that you may want to consider. The Mexican Government may have made inquiries in the United States to find the two families, but who told them they were here in out county. I did some checking and there's a family in Santa Ynez by the name of Hernandez, who are very close to the Consul Generale who came to our ranch.."

"I remember him and his Dragoon Captain."

"I believe that Hernandez told General Lopez that Robert and Jose were here. The Hernandez' sons made remarks about their

French heritage in front of several witnesses. I don't think they would've known about the two families unless Hernandez told them."

"What are you suggesting?"

Tommy smiled. "I think you can up the ante by charging Hernandez with conspiracy and subsequently General Lopez with conspiracy to commit murder and kidnapping. This whole episode has his fingerprints all over it. He came to our ranch to see if he could meet Robert and Jose while he was there. You may have a problem arresting the General unless he shows up for the trial. But he's as guilty as Diaz."

"The question is how do you get Lopez up here? I know it's a risk, but if you arrest the senior Hernandez and charge him with spying for Mexico, because that's what he may have done, he'll probably reach out to Lopez to get him out of trouble. What if Lopez bites and comes here, you could have Lopez in hand charged with whatever you decide,. The Mexican Government might be more receptive to a negotiation on terms that will stick."

"You certainly have a point. I have to think about this and do some studying to see if I could pull that off. Bringing Hernandez in is easy.

Lopez would be a problem unless he comes here. Maybe, arresting Hernandez for spying may make Lopez want to visit me?"

# CHAPTER 20

They'd received a telegram two days ago to expect their old friend James J. Jefferson and a colleague named Mike Cutler to stop by the ranch. The pair arrived about one in the afternoon and were greeted by Sarah Sanchez. "Tommy is fishing with Enrique Gutierrez and should be home around five. Can you two stay for dinner?"

"That would be nice. We'd like to stay overnight and talk to Tommy about doing some tracking for us. But first, I have a meeting with Juan at his office in Santa Ynez. Do you know what it's about?"

"I really don't know but everything these days is about the invasion by the Mexicans to kidnap Robert and Jose; it's probably about that. Jim, you take the guest room inside and Mike can take the one in the barn. Show him where it is please. Can you be back by five when Tommy returns?"

"I'll try. Do you mind if I leave Mike here; he just came off a long case and could use some sleep?

"No problem, introduce him to Tomas before you go."

The meeting between Jefferson and Juan was exactly about the Mexicans on trial. "Jim. They've brought in some high-powered attorneys from Washington with international law expertise. I know you have a lot of contacts and perhaps can identify one or two attorneys that may want to help me with that aspect of the case."

"There's a retired attorney in Los Angeles who practiced in Sacramento for many years. He's especially knowledgeable about international trade, but I know that he had put together some agreements between California and Mexico, so he should be able to help. He's a good friend of mine and may be looking for something to do. I know he's not happy in retired life. I'll wire him from the ranch and see if I can put the two of you together. His name is Joshua Black."

Juan told Jefferson about Tommy's suggestion to trap General Lopez by using Hernandez as bait. "He always travels with those six dragoons. How do you plan to handle them?" Jefferson asked.

"I think Tommy can handle the dragoons if I can entice Lopez to come to Santa Barbara. He may think he's immune to prosecution in this county because of his diplomatic immunity. The idea that we're charging Hernandez as a spy may cloud his judgment and he'll come. "My hope is that someone with international law experience could guide me through that pitfall.

"Boy are you living dangerous. If you could pull it off, it may be the clout you need to resolve this situation once and for all. I've met Diaz a couple of times before he was El Presidente and I didn't like him." Are you coming to dinner tonight at the ranch?"

"No, I have some work to do before I leave. Besides, Linda is in Santa Barbara with her folks and I'm staying at the hotel in town. I'm going down there first thing in the morning. Stop in and see me on your way back to Los Angeles and let me know about Mr. Black."

Enrique asked Tommy when they were at the farm visiting Robert and Jose, if they could go fishing sometime. He wanted to talk to him about something Tommy called him yesterday to see if he was available today.

It was around ten AM when Enrique arrived and they were at the pond by noon. They saluted each other with a glass of the wine Tommy brought and cast out their lines; Enrique caught the first fish. After catching six each, they'd looked forward to frying the fish tonight. "Tell me what the problem is?"

"You promise not to laugh at what I'm about to say."

"No, I can keep a straight face."

"I met a woman, who is very pretty, but there's just one problem; she's very young."

"What does she think about the May to September romance?"

"I haven't asked her yet, but when I kissed her, she was warm and returned my fervor, so I think she's receptive.

"Have you met her parents?"

"Yes and her father is my age, so I'm a little nervous at what he would say.'

"Believe me when I say I understand. I was once engaged to a woman who was about fifteen years younger than. I. Her father didn't object; in fact he encouraged the relationship. Ask the girl if she's interested and then speak to the father. He may want a mature man for his daughter."

"Whatever happened to the girl, if I may ask?"

"She was murdered and yes I went after the men who killed her and I caught them." I shiver went down Enrique back when he realized what a force Tommy Sanchez was. Thank god, he was my friend. Enrique thought.

Tommy knew that Jefferson was coming by but he didn't know when. As he and Enrique arrived at the main house, they were delighted to see Jefferson sitting on the front porch and the three walked into the kitchen where Sarah was working with Naomi. "

"We caught twelve trout that we're hoping to have for dinner. They're pretty good size." Tommy said

"I figured you'd be here about this time and would bring fish. Dinner will be ready in about an hour. Naomi and I can clean them. Enrique, you can clean up in the children's bathroom. You're staying for dinner, aren't you? Sarah asked; he smiled.

The two children, Helga and Tommy Jr. joined the six adults and after dinner Naomi put them to bed. The remaining five had another glass of wine and when Jefferson told them why he was here; Sarah cleaned off the table, but before she left the room she looked at Enrique. "It's getting late. Helga can sleep with Naomi and you can use her room," Enrique smiled at Sarah.

After the men lit up cigars, Jefferson talked to Enrique and Tommy. "There're some small gangs that roam the northern part of Mexico, crossing the border at will and causing destruction wherever they go. Up until now, they robbed travelers, but recently, they stepped up their game and are attacking banks and businesses across the border in Brownsville, Texas. The most vicious of the gangs is led by a thirty year old blacksmith from Mexico City who they call El Diablo. He's over six foot tall with a burly frame' he murders at will. There are five others who travel with him."

"The Texas rangers chased them to the northern part of Texas and then the gang disappeared. Two months ago, they showed up in Los Angles, shot up a saloon and robbed the patrons. We know they were in Ventura and Santa Barbara recently, because we had multiple reports from travelers, who'd been robbed by six bandits. Jacob Thunder's deputies got on their trail but lost them in the hills. The Pinkerton Agency was hired by the state of Texas to find and arrest El Diablo and his gang. We're also authorized to hire others as necessary. Since you're the best tracker I know, I've come to see if you'll help?"

"Where's the last place they were seen?" Tommy asked.

Jefferson took out a map and showed Tommy a place about fifteen miles southeast of Santa Barbara where they were last seen. Tommy looked up at Jefferson. "That's familiar territory. Could they have gone to Silas Smith's ranch and holed up?"

"If not, then it has to be close by Snith's place." Jefferson responded.

"If we left by noon tomorrow, we could be at Smith's farm by sundown, the day after tomorrow. We have enough supplies on hand in the barn for a week. We may be out longer than that and have to resupply someplace. There's plenty of game in the area and we could live off the land for another week if we need to. Your thoughts?" Tommy asked Jefferson.

"Wait a second. I want in. I have considerable experience in the Spanish Military in hunting deserters. I can help. Besides, there are six of them and only three of you." Enrique was looking at Tommy as he made his plea.

"It's fine by me. Jim Jefferson is leading this group. It's up to him."

Jefferson was quick to respond. "Mike and I will be happy to have you. Why don't you be in charge of the arms and ammunition?" Enrique nodded his acceptance.

Sarah and Naomi, as usual were way ahead of the men. First thing in the morning they were up preparing food that six men would take with them. Tommy got Jefferson's permission to add two of the ranch's vaqueros to go along and handle the two mules that would haul supplies.

The six left at noon the next day and by sundown on the second day they were near the top of the hills overlooking the former Silas Smith ranch. Using binoculars, Jefferson made a visual sweep of the farm; it appeared to be deserted. The vaqueros were experienced in setting up camp and soon they had a fire going and dinner prepared. Sarah and Naomi had cut six steaks the morning they left and their first meal was steak and baked potatoes. They knew that the rest of the fare wouldn't be as elegant but all six were happy. Jefferson established four-hour shifts for two men each on sentry duty at night. They kept the farm in view the entire night.

# CHAPTER 21

Silas Smith had leased his one thousand acre spread to a couple from Oregon, with an option to buy. When the six members of the Jefferson party reached the farm, they couldn't find anyone on the property. They checked the barn, the storage unit and then the house. There were dirty dishes in the sink and on the counter next to it. Dried bread was on the table and at least two beds had been slept in. Men's clothes were strewn on the floor and a significant number of candlesticks and silver platters were in a bag in one of the corners of the kitchen. Cigarette butts were all over the floor. "I think El Diablo and his crew have been using the farm as a hideout." Tommy said.

"I wonder what happened to the Oregon couple who leased the place. Either they left or there may be foul play here. We should keep an eye out for bodies or soft ground." Jefferson responded.

"I know someone who would know what's going on. There're three Indians living in a shack that work the farm. It's only about two miles. If you can spare me, I'll ride over and see what they have to say."

It took him a little over an hour to ride over to their place. The woman who spoke a little English, indicated the couple who leased the place had left for Santa Barbara after six bandits knocked on their door and demanded food. The couple gave them food but that didn't deter the bandits from stealing supplies in their barn and sleeping there. The couple feared for their life and left while the bandits were asleep. They've been gone three days The Indian Woman indicated the bandits were still in the area.

When Tommy returned and reported to Jefferson, the group decided to go back to the barn and set up camp for the night. They kept two on alert near the pond, two near the trail they used leading into the farm and two in the barn. One of each pair would sleep while the other stood watch.

The next morning Tommy and Enrique found tracks leading from the cabin going southeast. They were careful of an ambush by El Diablo and took their time following the tracks. After ten miles, they hid behind some rocks to rest while they watched the trail. "You know, it's possible the group moved on." Enrique offered.

"It's possible, then again they have a good hideout at the farm and may want to use it as a staging place to raid the other farms and ranches in the area. You remember the four sacks of silver in the kitchen. They're not going o leave that behind if they can help it. If they leave for another place, I'll find them."

Over the next two days, Tommy and Enrique extended their distance from the farm and discovered that the bandits used the route to come back to the farm on at least two occasions in the past. "My guess is they may come back to the farm sometime in the next few days if they come at all. Let's go back and talk to the others. Jefferson is in charge and may have some thoughts." Tommy said.

Though it was getting colder at night, Jefferson felt a fire could be seen too far away, so they had a cold dinner and discussed what action they should take. Tommy was the first to speak. "I think they're coming back here in a few days. This is a good hideout, no one comes here; it's too isolated. Lenny Harris who masterminded the Oxnard train robbery used it for years. The only reason Jefferson and I found him living here, was because we followed the woman he was living home."

"You have good instincts. What do you suggest?" Jefferson asked Tommy.

"I say we wait two more nights but move up to the lake. There's less chance of being surprised up there and there's plenty of trees and logs that we can use if there's a shootout. I think Enrique and I ought to go out early the next two mornings to see if we can come up on them, especially if they're heading back this way. If we don't see them or if they get past us, we'll be in a position to come up behind them if they return to the farm."

The next two days were uneventful though Tommy and Enrique extended their area of investigation by two miles each day. They started back to the farm around two in the afternoon. As they came over the ridge above the farm, they could hear gunshots fired from below. They knew that Jefferson and the other three were well-armed, could shoot and had established good defensive positions.

They eased their way down the slope and approached the cabin, but the shooting was heavy up by the pond nearly three hundred yards south of their position. They tied their horses to the rail in front of the house and Tommy went around one side of the house while Enrique took the other. They crouched as they made their way up the slight rise maintaining a ten-foot distance between them as they moved from log to log making their way toward the pond.

Jefferson and the others were behind some trees about forty yards east of the pond. Tommy could see four men with their backs to them as he and Enrique starting shooting at them, the bandits were caught between the two groups. Tommy couldn't tell where the other two bandits were, but assumed they were to the east of Jefferson's position.

Enrique was an excellent shot and hit one of the bandits in the head and he dropped to the ground. The other three between Jefferson and Tommy turned and opened up on Tommy and Enrique. Tommy wounded one and he fell where he was. Enrique killed another and soon three horsemen broke from the trees, raced toward the cabin and then to the trail they'd been using.

Jefferson and the others came out of the trees and joined up with the Tommy and Enrique. "Jim, we have them on the run, let's get them now." Tommy said.

Tommy, "I'd like to leave your two vaqueros here to see about the wounded man and bury the other two while the four of us go after them."

"Let's go." Tommy, Enrique, Jefferson and Mike Cutler rushed to the cabin, got on their horses and went after the three bandits; Tommy was in the lead. They followed fresh tracks and occasionally could see the riders up ahead. As darkness started to fall, they had to find a place to hole up for the night. "How far do you think we're behind?" Jefferson asked Tommy

"No more than a half hour. We can take our time. If they try to get further ahead, their horses will break down.  Although we have the upper hand, my main concern is that they may try to set up an ambush. Let's keep two men on sentry duty with four hour shifts and leave at first light."

El Diablo and the other two members of his gang were exhausted. Two of them wanted to stop for the night but the boss man wouldn't hear of it.  He wanted to increase the distance between them and the pursuers; his men had to ride through the night.

Tommy had tracked many Indians, bandits and escaped prisoners. The one thing he learned while tracking these people was that the pursuers had to have patience. His success rate was one hundred percent. Each of the four in his group had a least four hours sleep and they were ready the next morning. Tommy took the point and followed the tracks of the three killers. He noticed one of the horses had started to limp and knew it was only a matter of time before the others would leave him.

They followed the same procedure as the day and night before and in the morning they were ready to finish the job. Around noon, they found one of the bandits lying along the trail. He'd been shot in the heart. His horse was caught in the bushes. Enrique freed the horse and checked his shoes. There was a rock lodged in the right front shoe. When that was removed, the horse was able to move freely without a limp. At day's end they found a place to camp and ate some of the beef jerky that Sarah provided.

Soon after they started to chase the bandits the next morning, they were fired on from a small hill just to the right of the trail they were following. None of them were hit, but they grabbed their rifles and were out of the saddle immediately, seeking cover. Tommy motioned for them to spread out and encircle the bandits. "Take your time. They're not going anyplace."

The four fired continuously at the remaining two outlaws. After thirty minutes one rider raced off. The four lawmen walked up the hill and found one of the bandits lying on his side. Tommy checked for a pulse; there was none. He'd been shot in the head. They freed the two horses of the dead Mexicans. The two Pinkertons stayed with the dead Mexican and their two horses. Tommy and Enrique raced after the last rider; it was El Diablo.

The burly Mexican tried to outrace the two, but they were only one hundred yards behind and closing quickly. Enrique was firing his rifle from the saddle and soon El Diablo's horse was hit and the rider fell to the ground. They dismounted and immediately came under fire from a clump of bushes near where the rider fell. Tommy waved at Enrique and when the Spaniard gave a thumbs up, Tommy circled to his right and came up behind El Diablo. "In Spanish, Tommy said, "You have a choice. You can die here or we'll take you back across one of the saddles."

El Diablo turned quickly, but the son of Sitting Bull was too quick and he fired two shots at El Diablo and the gunman fell to the ground; he'd been hit the shoulder twice. Tommy disarmed the Mexican and called for Enrique. The only thing that the surviving killer had to say, was, "you'll never get me back to Mexico. I'm going to kill all of you."

El Diablo was a formidable-looking opponent, but with his hands handcuffed behind his back, he was at an extreme disadvantage. They buried the two bandits who were killed and made their way back to Silas Smith's leased farm. El Diablo tried to escape a couple of times but the two vaqueros tied his legs to a metal stake near the barn and El Diablo became easier to deal with. Even so, it took an extra day to reach Santa Barbara because Tommy and Enrique went hunting and brought back a buck to supplement their diet. The vaqueros cooked the venison over an open fire and even El Diablo enjoyed the feast.

Paterson and his companion left the other four, took El Diablo with them and caught the Oxnard train. The two Pinkerton Detectives had no problem handling the Mexican and he was turned over to the Texas Rangers who came by train to Los Angeles. Patterson learned later that El Diablo was hung in Brownsville Texas.

As Tommy and Enrique were returning through Santa Barbara, they notified the sheriff that they had captured El Diablo and that the renters of Silas Smith's property could return to their farm.

# CHAPTER 22

Over the past month, Juan Sanchez has been under fire from the US State Department, the Mexican Government and attorneys from the Us Attorney General's Office. Many attorneys seem to have taken up residence in Santa Barbara. Some were sent by The President's staff to make sure Juan knew how the Feds felt about this trial. Throughout this interference, Juan was moving forward with his case and politely ignoring all the outside advice he was getting. Thankfully, the local newspaper was on his side and their editorials chastised meddlesome outsiders. "Let the man do his job" was the headline this week.

Juan was more comfortable the last two days, because his main confidant had returned from helping capture El Diablo. In addition to his step-father, Joshua Black arrived after he and Juan traded letters for a few weeks. According to Black, "I'm here to help you as much as I can. We can beat the bastards."

Blacks resume was unique. He was an Irish Seaman, who studied the law in Ireland, then came to California and finished his law training at the University of California. It was when he moved to Los Angeles that he became acquainted with several Mexican Businessmen who'd been having a difficult time selling their products to the State of California. Black learned his trade by the "trial and error method" and within a few years, his practice boomed. In his most recent years before he retired, he was the Assistant Attorney General for the State of California, overseeing the International Sale's Division..

Juan knew the Federal Government's position was not without merit. The US Secretary of State officially handles negotiations between countries. That's why Juan insisted that the ten Mexican Soldiers only be tried on state charges. He wondered down deep if he could really go to trial.

The main problem was how to stop the Mexicans from sending hit squads whenever they wanted. He talked this over with Tommy Sanchez to see what his read on the situation was.

"I think you're correct. If you don't penalize them for sending hit squads, they'll feel embolden. The only thing I can think of that will curtail Mexico is to have them found guilty and hung. One of the problems it creates is that Mexico can pick up any American in their country, trump up some fake charges and hang them. The cure could be worse than the disease."

"There's also the option of a financial penalty so steep, that they'll think more than twice before they send anyone. If I could give you any advice, it would be that you should keep going as you are, but let it be known that you would negotiate if the incentive was there. Let them make the overtures. They'll avoid it as long as possible, so you have to create a situation that forces them to want to talk."

"As usual, you see it clearly. I have a real concern that the federal government may send troops and preclude any chance of negotiation." Juan responded.

"If they send troops, they'll not send an army. My guess is they'll send a token force and house them in the Presidio. We can raise many more men than that and force them to back down. We have enough ranchers and cowboys that would wall them in so they couldn't come out. If I was them, I wouldn't play that card. People would get hurt and perhaps an election lost. We love our country, but don't want the Federal Government to interfere with us locally unless absolutely necessary. This isn't one of those times. What about the people who gave you this job?"

"So far, they're fully behind me. They're mostly rich ranchers and the power players in the county.  But they're used to getting their way. What happens when the Federal Government tells them to back off?  Will they still be behind me? The governor is my main concern and he has a national guard that he can use. He hasn't come out in the open yet but he's a member of the same party in power in Washington DC  I expect to have his aide visit me any time now. How about dinner tonight at The Cave.? You haven't been there since I bought the restaurant."

"Your mother is with me and I'm sure she'd be delighted to see you. Where's Linda?'

"Since I'm putting so much time on the case against the Mexicans, she's with me in Santa Barbara full time. She not really showing yet, but I'm more comfortable that she's with me. Shall we say the four of us meet at seven o'clock at the restaurant?"

They were staying at the Arlington Hotel and when Tommy told Sarah about dinner with Linda and her son, she was delighted. They rented a carriage and driver and were at the restaurant by seven in the evening. The restaurant was full and Juan met them at the door and escorted them to a table where Linda was sitting.

They drank a bottle of wine and ordered dinner. Juan had made some changes to the restaurant, notably the addition of a guitarist who entertained the patrons during dinner. When the guitarist came to their table, Sarah asked Tommy to dance with her. There was a small section where one or two couples could comfortably dance and Tommy took her hand and led her there. They were a handsome couple but she was a blond beauty. Many of the patrons turned and stared at the couple. When the music ended Tommy led her back to the table and Juan kissed his mother on the cheek.

There were several Washington attorneys and a couple of US Senators that Juan noted sitting at a table on the far wall. The four finished dinner and were having after-dinner drinks when one of the men sitting with the Washington Attorneys rose and made his way to The Sanchez' table. "I'm Senator Jack Hunter of Oregon. I remember being at a ball in Washington that was in honor of Crazy Horse, the Indian Warlord who murdered General Custer and all his men." The four Sanchez' at the table wondered what would come next.

"I danced with a beautiful blonde woman that night who was the wife of Crazy Horse. Might you be that woman?" he asked as he looked directly at Sarah.

"I was there and danced with many dignitaries but I don't recall dancing with you Senator. "

Juan rose. I don't think this is appropriate Senator. I must ask you to leave."

"Not before I dance with the pretty lady. Give me your hand madam?"

Tommy Sanchez rose and there was silence in the restaurant; many recognized the famed gunman. "My wife does not recall meeting you Senator, nor will she dance with you this evening. You're a nuisance and I ask you politely to leave our table. In addition, the owner has asked you to leave. Please honor his request."

Senator Hunter smiled, walked back to his table, said something to his two guests and all three left the restaurant.

"Boy, was that ever close." Juan said

"I don't think it's ended. My guess is that the senator and his friends are outside waiting for us to exit. Juan, you know what I need. I won't need it long because the carriage has what I need."

When it was time to leave, The four family members walked out the front door and saw the senator and his two friends sitting in their carriage. When their driver saw Tommy exit the restaurant, he turned to the senator and his friends. "Gentlemen, that's Tommy Sanchez, the most feared gunman in California. I can see he has a gun at his side. Let me take you to your hotel. He's not someone you want to provoke."

"Not until I've had my dance." The senator said as he stepped down from his carriage and walked up to the four.

"I didn't want to make a scene inside so I waited here. Madam, I know there's no music, but I would be honored if you would grant me a dance."

Sarah made a slight movement and Tommy frowned at her. "My wife is tired. I suggest you and your friends leave us. This can only end badly for you."

"Oh, I've heard about you but I'm not the least bit intimidated. I'm gong to have that dance or one of us will be dead. Do you understand?"

No sooner had Senator Hunter uttered those words, when Juan, Linda and Sarah moved six feet to the left of Tommy, who moved his coat back exposing his gun and holster.

The senator moved one pace closer to Tommy and like him exposed a gun and holster. His two colleagues stayed in the carriage. The driver put his head in his lap. Senator Hunter moved slightly, cried out and grabbed his left ear. Blood was pouring from the bullet wound he suffered. His two companions rushed to his side, but the senator put out his hand to stop them and went for his gun again. He screamed; it was as though his right ear exploded in blood.

By this time one of the senator's companions pressed handkerchiefs to both of his ears to stop the flow of blood while his other companion took away his gun and threw it in the street. "You better take the senator to the hospital; I'll notify the sheriff of the incident." Juan told the driver.

The two companions helped Senator Hunter into the carriage and they sped off to the hospital. Juan roused Jacob Thunder and told him what happened and who the participants were. Juan spent the next hour taking statements from those who viewed the incident. Most saw it the same way; another thought Tommy was the instigator.

The two couples went their separate ways but agreed to meet in Juan's Santa Barbara Office at ten the next morning. Linda was quite upset that their evening turned bad. She asked Juan what would happen.

"Hopefully, the senator will wake up and want to leave as soon as possible and put this behind him."

The ride back to the Arlington was strained. Tommy was quiet and Sarah knew he was angry that she made a move to dance with the senator.

# CHAPTER 23

The newspaper headlines were bold. "Senator shot in both ears." The story went on to state that the senator insisted upon dancing with another man's wife and the husband took exception. The shooter was Tommy Sanchez of Santa Ynez, the rest of the story narrated what bystanders saw. A supplementary article went on to tell the story of Tommy Sanchez; from his early life as a Sioux Brave to the Businessman he is today. There was no mention of his service to the community.

Jacob Thunder, the Sheriff of Santa Barbara County was waiting for Sarah and Tommy as they entered Juan's office. They told him what happened inside the restaurant and what also happened outside.

"Had you met the Senator before?" Thunder asked Sarah.

"Not that I'm aware of. He seemed to think I had when I went to Washington with my first husband, Crazy Horse."

"Had you met Senator Hunter before?" Jacob asked Tommy.

"No, I never have."

"I applaud your discretion and skill. We don't need a dead senator in our town. I'm going to the hospital and get a statement from Senator Hunter. Do you want to come along Juan?"

"It might not hurt to see what we're going to face. Mom, can you and Tommy stay another day in town. I know you both like the Arlington, so I'll come by after I see the senator." Sarah looked at Tommy who nodded his agreement.

The press was all over the hospital waiting for a statement form Senator Hunter. This was big news. The reporters were held in the lobby but the sheriff and Juan walked through the gauntlet and made their way to the senator's room. The doctor was just finishing his analysis and was leaving the senator's room as Thunder and Juan Sanchez approached. . His two friends from last evening were leaning against the wall in the hallway, opposite the senator's door. Juan learned from the doctor that the two friends were Congressman James Spicer and Congressman Wayne Jeffers. Each represented a separate district in Oregon.

The sheriff introduced himself and Juan Sanchez to Senator Hunter. "Who are you?" Hunter asked Juan.

"I'm the owner of the restaurant where you dined last evening."

"Who shot me?" Hunter asked the sheriff.

"A man named Thomas Sanchez of Santa Ynez. He's a well-respected man in this area and owner of a large ranch where he grows grapes and raises cattle. "

"Where was he standing when he shot me?"

"He was standing in front of you."

"That's impossible. The man in front of me didn't move. I was ambushed by someone in the shadows. Did you at least investigate who it could be? I have some enemies,"

'There were at least six eyewitnesses to the confrontation between you and Mr. Sanchez. It was he who shot at your ears."

"That's impossible. I'm pretty handy with a gun, having survived three duels. The man in front of me never moved toward his gun. I was shot by someone else."

"Tommy Sanchez is the fastest man alive when drawing and firing his handgun. I've seen him in operation and it was exactly as you described. I don't know why he's so much faster than anyone else. Perhaps he watches his opponent's eyes: perhaps it's intuitive. Whatever the reason, he's that fast and he did shoot at both your ears. It's his calling card so to speak."

"My friends tell me that I was somewhat of an asshole last night and I insulted Mrs. Sanchez. If what you say is true, I'd like to have this all go away. Is that possible?"

"I think all of us would like to see this go away. We have a lot on our plate with The Mexican incursion. Mr. Juan Sanchez is the lead prosecutor on the case. Tommy Sanchez is his stepfather."

"Do you think its possible to meet Mr. Sanchez?"

"I'll ask but I can't promise you. The woman you tried to dance with is my mother. My step-father is very sensitive to how people treat my mother."

"I've got a few hours of questions from the press. It would help if Sanchez would cooperate and help bail me out." Senator Hunter said.

Jacob Thunder went back to his office and Juan went to the Arlington to meet with his mother and step-father. On the way out of the hospital, they were pushed and shoved by the reporters making their way to the senator's room. The two elder Sanchez' were in the dining room when Juan arrived.

"How did it go?" Juan's mother asked.

"Better than I expected, though he doesn't believe you shot him. He thinks he was fired upon from ambush, because he never saw you move. I believe it when he said he wants this to go away. He'd like to meet with you Tommy. I told him I wasn't sure you would. I think it would be good publicity if you were photographed shaking hands. Mom, I don't advise you get involved."

"Normally, I wouldn't meet with someone who wanted to shoot me, but if you think it would make this situation disappear, I will meet with him. I'm not convinced that he won't try to get even. I wouldn't want to stumble into a situation that could get out of hand. Why don't we meet where you and the sheriff can be present?"

"That should work. Let me see what I can do. What's good here?"

"The scallops are their specialty" Tommy said.

They met in the sheriff's office. The senator brought his two congressional friends. Hunter apologized for his behavior and asked if he could make his apologies directly to Mrs. Sanchez.

"That's not possible senator. I accept your apology on her and my behalf. I hope that you have a nice trip home." Tommy walked out the building and got in his carriage
All three congressmen shook Juan's hand and stated that they were heading home this afternoon.

Sarah was at the Arlington, sitting in the lobby reading a magazine when Tommy returned. He told her the affair was over and the congressmen were heading home. "Tell me, did you ever dance with the senator?"

"I was so young at that time and this was the biggest event I'd ever attended. I did dance with a lot of men, but I don't remember any of them."

As she lay alongside her husband that evening, Sarah remembered the night of the ball in the nation's capitol. She remembered dancing with the senator. It was he who kept squeezing her bottom while they were on the dance floor. She pulled away from him and said something that only he could hear. "My husband, Crazy Horse has scalped twenty men. I dare not think what he would do if I told him you were taking liberties with me."

The senator thanked her for the dance and left the auditorium immediately. She didn't dare tell Tommy the story. He probably would have killed the senator. As it was, the senator received an appropriate rebuke that made up for the lack of one in Washington.. She was sure when he sobered up, he would realize how lucky he was to get away so easy.

# CHAPTER 24

Over a two day period, Juan met with Sheriff Thunder to come up with a strategy in dealing with the Hernandez family. Juan felt the father told General Lopez where Robert St. Pierre was.. They weren't sure they could prove it, but they did learn that Mr. and Mrs. Fowler, a grain supplier to Rancho Del Prado were at the Sanchez' Christmas Party. When Hernandez subsequently came to his warehouse, Fowler told him about the wonderful party he attended. Mr. Hernandez asked Fowler if there were any French people attending. Fowler said there was a Robert St. Pierre and family. Hernadez asked him how old Robert was and Fowler said he was about 45-50 years old.

They decided that Thunder and two deputies would get a warrant to have the father come to the Santa Barbara jail to answer questions. Ernesto Hernandez was shocked that he was served a warrant to answer the sheriff's questions. He arrived on time with a local attorney he hired. His attorney was surprised that Juan Sanchez was present and that Hernandez was sworn in and told what his rights were.

With the sheriff present, Juan went through a list of questions he'd prepared. If Hernandez wasn't nervous before, the first question made him squirm in his chair. "How well do you know General Lopez, the Consul Generale of Mexico?"

Hernadez' attorney objected. "Who says he knows the General?"

Juan produced the photo of the two families in the carriage taken during the Cinco de Maio Parade in Santa Barbara. "I think it's evident,

"Were you aware that the Mexican Government was planning an incursion into our county to kidnapped Robert St. Pierre and Jose Santana and take them back to Mexico?"

"No, I did not" The sweat was pouring down Hernandez' face as he answered.

"We think you did and that you spied for the Mexican Government and therefore are guilty of treason."

Hernandez started to convulse and nearly threw up. His attorney asked for a few minutes to talk to his client. Juan didn't overhear the conversation, but he knew what they were saying to each other. When the questioning continued, Hernandez said to Juan, "upon advice from counsel, I will not answer anymore questions for fear that I might implicate myself."

"That's certainly is your prerogative. Ernesto Hernandez, You are under arrest. I'm charging you with spying for a foreign government and conspiracy to assist a foreign government in the overthrow of our government. I intend to seek the death penalty."

Hernandez' attorney was angry. "This is nothing but a witch hunt. You can't get away with this. I'll see that you're disbarred."

Sheriff Thunder served the warrant, read Hernandez his rights, placed him under arrest and took him into custody. His attorney wasn't finished. "You can't get away with harassing normal citizens. He's no more a spy than you are. This is just a ploy on you part to gain some leverage.'

"Sir, I can assure you I'm serious. This invasion by the Mexican Government was initiated when Hernandez told General Lopez about Santana and St, Pierre. Americans were killed as a result of his actions. I intend to prove that he was an agent of the Mexican Government. You better believe I'm serious."

The trial of the Mexicans charged with murder, attempted murder, conspiracy and kidnapping was scheduled for Monday, two weeks hence, Juan decided to try Hernandez for spying for a foreign government and for conspiracy to commit kidnapping. He petitioned the court for a trial date.

Juan and Black felt that Hernandez was part of the overall conspiracy to kidnap Robert and Jose, but all his time for the near future was on the incursion. He spent the past month interviewing all the witnesses and arranging for accommodations for them for a week. One of the surprises was the arrival of John Wroster, the former Under- Secretary of State, who negotiated with the Mexican Government to settle the issue in New Mexico. John Wroster became a fountain of information for Juan and he felt very comfortable going to trial. The main thing he shared with Juan was the fact that the Mexicans negotiated very hard. They felt the Americans would give in, so why make serious proposals. "If I had it to do over again, I would have insisted on reparations for the two families as a starter." Wroster said.

On the opposite side, the State Department had ratcheted up their involvement. They established offices in one of the building on State Street across from the Mexican Delegation's offices. There were times during the trial preparation when Juan felt he was a sole attorney fighting against two countries. Representatives for both countries came on a daily basis without appointments. Finally, Juan set a time frame of two hours a week on each Thursday to hear their opinions.

He'd been expecting a visit and finally the top aides to the governor and state attorney general came on a Monday. To their credit they scheduled an appointment with Juan and just didn't walk in as did the federal government representatives.

The two aides told Juan they'd just come from Washington and wanted to talk about an alternative to a trial.

"What do you have in mind?" Jun asked as he was sitting at his desk and both men were in chairs facing him.

Their names were Frank Wilson from the governor's office and Charles Dane from the State Attorney General.

"Everyone thinks you have a good case and have pursued it in a professional manner. But the governor thinks it's time to turn it over to the feds and have them work out a reasonable solution." Wilson said.

"I assume you've had considerable discussion with our cousins from Washington. You've wasted your time in our nation's capitol. I could've told you what they want. In fact you could've gone across the street and asked them. They're here in mass." Juan asked.

"As a matter of fact, Charlie and I just came from a meeting with the fed attorneys across the street."

"Well then, what is a reasonable solution?"

"We're not prepared to make public those positions. Dane said.

"Well gentleman, until you're willing to speak plainly with me and give me something I think is reasonable, those fourteen Mexicans are going to trial next week and I'm going to ask for the death penalty."

"You can't do that, you don't have the authority." Dane said

"Oh, I have the authority. The people of Santa Barbara County are angry and they want a conviction. They murdered two of Mrs. Cota's vaqueros; she wants a conviction. Jose Santana's daughter was kidnapped and roughed up. He and his wife want a conviction. But most of all, the people of this county want to know how in hell, when the same thing happened in New Mexico, why the Federal Government wants to let the Mexicans go free. That's not going to happen here."

"We can send troops and take the Mexicans from you."

"That point has already been addressed by the county supervisors. The consensus is that the ranchers in the area could field one thousand cowboys on a moment's notice to defend our county. When we had a train robbery a couple of years ago, we had over one hundred fifty men who volunteered to join the posse to track seven bandits. Tell the governor that's a lot of votes in a close election."

"Come on Juan. You're not being realistic. Give us something we can bring back to our superiors and maybe we can help if you have a political career in mind." Wilson smiled.

"I don't have any political ambitions. My concern is what my supervisors in the county have directed me to do. Has the governor considered what this is doing to the two families? What do you plan to tell them when you let the Mexicans go free?"

"We have an ambivalent feeling toward St. Pierre and Santana. They did kill border guards as they were escaping. We're not suggesting that the Mexicans go scot free. We're just not willing to lay all our cards on the table."

You've given me nothing. Why don't you make a reasonable attempt at something this county can consider. If you want me to take the first step, you're wasting your time." Juan stood up signaling the two men that their time was up.

# CHAPTER 24

General Lopez was livid when he found out that Hernandez had been arrested and charged with spying for the Mexicans. He called the Governor's office and spoke to the governor's chief of staff. The man said he would notify the governor and look into the situation. When he didn't hear back after three days, he wired President Diaz and informed him of the situation. Three days later he wired his president again. After another week, he knew that neither the Governor of California nor the President of Mexico was going to intercede.

He called in Captain Suarez of his Dragoons and told him about the charges against Ernesto Hernandez, who was Suarez' cousin. He asked him if it was possible for he and his men to slip into Santa Barbara and rescue Hernandez. "Will I have diplomatic immunity if I'm caught?"

"I will use all the power of my office to see that you have it, but the prosecutor is not listening to anyone but his father, so I can't guarantee you that I can intercede. So the answer is no."

"There is no doubt in my mind that the seven of us can get into Santa Barbara without being recognized. Additionally, we can certainly get out without too much concern. The problem that we can't foresee is what happens when we try to take Hernandez out of their jail? Sir, the other concern I have is, will they be waiting for us. Is Hernadez nothing more than bait to trap you?"

"I agree that he could be bait but my problem is, if we don't rescue him, he may become frustrated and turn on me. I could be indicted for planning the incursion.. As long as I'm in Los Angeles, I'm safe but if I should go near Santa Barbara, there's no telling what the prosecutor might do. The more dangerous person is his step-father."

"Sir, I could send one of my men to check out the jail and see where it's vulnerable. With that information, we could make a better decision."

The Consul Generale sat with his head in his hands and thought for a few seconds. "If you have someone you can trust and is smart enough not to get caught, do it."

Francisco Medina knew what his orders were with particular emphasis on not being caught. He dressed as a vaquero, took the train to Santa Barbara and checked into a medium-priced hotel on lower State Street. The jail was nearby, so the next morning he walked by the jail to see how many deputies were on duty.

There were a significant number of people milling around outside trying to get a glimpse of the Mexican prisoners. Francisco learned from overhearing the visitors talking to each other, that those prisoners were in a makeshift jail behind the regular jail. The only access to them was through the jail's front door.

There was an outdoor restaurant across from the jail where people sat trying to see what was going on. Francisco wanted to find out when a shift change was made and how many guards would be on duty at one time. It took him two days but he was comfortable that shift changes were made at seven in the morning and seven in the evening and that there were six guards on duty at all times. Although there was no rear exit to the jail area where the Mexican Soldiers were being held, there was an alley that went behind that area. Without being seen, he paced off the distances around the jail compound.

The next morning, he returned to Los Angeles and met with his superior and General

Lopez. Prior to that meeting, Francisco drew up a map of the jail from what he saw, what he measured and what several bystanders were able to provide. The three talked for thirty minutes. Finally, Lopez asked the two if Hernandez could be rescued.

Francisco responded. "I'm not sure if he can be rescued but I can tell you a way that it might be done."

"Go ahead." Lopez said.

"I would create a diversion around one AM. One man would throw some sort of incendiary device into the compound from the alley behind. This is where the makeshift cells for our Mexican Soldiers are located. This device should alert all the guards and they'll probably rush to that area. My guess is they'd think someone was trying to free our soldiers. Simultaneously, two or three men could rush the front door or break it down, find Hernandez and make their way out. I would have three more of our men near the front door to neutralize any guards that wanted to follow. The total number of men required would be seven. They would ride horses directly from Los Angeles to Santa Barbara. On the way back they'd use the uninhabited areas southeast of Santa Barbara as cover.

"Couldn't the incendiary device kill our own soldiers in the makeshift cells?" Lopez asked.

"We'd have to be sure what is thrown in doesn't have that much force. We could build some sort of enclosure with makeshift cells out in the country and practice throwing charges until we get it correct. It's my understanding that this exercise is only to free Hernandez?" Lopez nodded his head yes.

Time was of the essence, so they found a place in the country, east of Los Angeles to build the enclosure. They practiced for a day using dummies to replicate the soldiers. When they thought they had it correct, Captain Suraez and his dragoons would take the train to Ventura the following day, offloaded their mounts and made their way north. They were traveling light, carrying only side arms, with minimum ammunition, water and an extra horse for Hernandez. The day before they left they selected a town forty miles east of Santa Barbara, called Mira Monte as a resupply location. It was north of Ventura and should be easy to access and resupply Suarez and his group. General Lopez's staff would leave by train so they'd get to Mira Monte, before Suarez.

After the Suarez Group arrived in Santa Barbara, they assembled on the outskirts of the city and went over the plan one more time. They left so that they'd be at the jail shortly before one AM. The individual selected to thrown the incendiary was first to depart followed by the three with sledgehammers to break down the front door of the jail. The last group to include Captain Suarez would provide cover for the three plus Hernandez coming out of the jail; however, they left one dragoon to tend the eight horses.

As soon as the incendiary was thrown, the guards rushed to see what the problem was and protect the  Mexican Prisoners in their cells. Three dragoons broke down the front door and rushed in. They quickly found keys and went into the normal cell area and called out Hernandez name. When he yelled, they opened his cell and the four rushed out the front door. Two of the jail guards saw what was happening and rushed to intercept Hernandez and the three dragoons. They were beaten back by Suarez and a dragoon providing cover. They shot the two guards and off they went to where the horses were being tended. The seven dragoons and Hernandez mounted their horses and rode east.

The sheriff was called immediately. When he saw the damage, his two guards wounded and loss of an inmate, he wired Tommy Sanchez at his ranch. Tommy was asleep and got the message the next morning. He called Enrique and Silas and they arrived within an hour. Tomas had prepared supplies for five days and Tommy, four of his vaqueros and his two friends were ready by nine in the morning and off they went to the Santa Barbara Jail.

They arrived at the jail by two in the afternoon and were met by Sheriff Thunder. "Tommy, they have over a twelve hour start and may be resupplied somewhere in the mountains, so be careful. If at all possible, we need to find out who's behind this. I want them back alive. I want to swear in all your people as deputies and I'm sending two of mine with you under your command."

"Jacob, I give you my word that we'll try to bring all of them back alive, if possible. Why not wire the Pinkertons and see if they know anything about this and where they might be resupplied." Thunder acknowledged.

The two most experienced people in this posse were Tommy Sanchez and Enrique Contreras. Both knew that they'd needed to take their time, even though they were twelve hours behind.

Tommy addressed the posse before they departed. "I feel comfortable that we'll catch them. They are looking at long jail terms, so they're probable desperate. Don't take any chances and we'll all come home alive and safe."

Before they left Santa Barbara, they found where the eight horses were tended during the attack on the jail. They were able to follow the Dragoons and Hernandez clearly. After coffee and some biscuits that Sarah prepared, they were on their way. Since Tommy was the skilled tracker, he rode point most of the way with Silas bringing up the rear. Occasionally, Tommy would ride ahead and then wait until the group caught up. He estimated they narrowed the distance to six hours after the first day. Tommy and his group stopped at eight in the evening and posted one guard. By the third day, he felt that they were only three hours behind and should catch them in two days even if they were resupplied.

Suraez was an infantry soldier turned Dragoon. The last few years were spent guarding General Lopez. It was good duty but after two days of riding, he was exhausted as were the other Dragoons and his second in command asked is they could rest a half day. He heart told him to acquiesce; however, his military background told him to rest when they were safe. They definitely were not safe. He couldn't tell if they sent troops after him, but that didn't matter. He had to assume they did. "Lieutenant Padea, we cannot rest until we reach Los Angeles and are on a ship bound for Vera Cruz."

On the fourth day, the pursuers saw lights in the distance and assumed Suarez and his group were heading to one of the towns north of Ventura, near lake Casitas. Tommy talked it over with Enrique, Silas and Tomas. They decided to travel through the night to see if they could catch the men they were chasing. His vaqueros were a hearty lot and could easily go without sleep if necessary.

With Tommy in the lead they made it to the outskirts of the town of Mira Monte by four in the morning. They figured that Suarez and his men arrived at midnight and were probably asleep. They circled the town before light trying to find the group. Around six in the morning, Tomas reported that he knew where twelve men were camped. They followed him and spread out as they approached the camp. When they were sure if was the men they were after, they encircled the group. There was one sentry, but he was sound asleep. Tommy recognized Suarez who was sleeping on his stomach and stuck his rifle in the Mexican's back. Suarez came up quickly and yelled out. Most of his men reached for their weapons, but Tomas and the vaqueros fired a dozen shots close to all the soldiers to discourage them. They all sat up but remained still.

"Captain Suarez, you're under arrested for breaking into the Santa Barbara Jail and escaping with Ernesto Hernandez. We're taking you back to Santa Barbara to stand trial. I gave my word to the sheriff that I would try to bring you back alive, but that's your choice. Each of my men is an excellent shot and will kill you if necessary. Do you understand?" Suarez nodded his understanding.

Tomas and the vaqueros disarmed all twelve of the captured men and tied their hands behind them. They gathered up all the guns and ammunition and bought two burros from a local farmer to carry the excess supplies.

"Who are these four men?" Tommy pointed to the staff members of General Lopez.

"Why don't you ask them yourself?" Suarez wasn't going to be cooperative
Tommy left that chore to Enrique, who was very aggressive in his questioning of the men. He eventually found out that they were here to

resupply Captain Suarez and assist him in any way they could. Tommy wired Sheriff Thunder that they captured twelve men including Hernandez, with no casualties on either side. They were going to return by horse to Ventura and then by train to Santa Barbara. When Thunder got the wire, he notified Sarah and Silas' wife.

Thunder commandeered the train from Santa Barbara to Ventura and was waiting when Tommy and the others arrived. The four deputies he brought with him took over guarding the twelve so Tommy and his group could relax. There was a short delay in Ventura while they turned the engine toward Santa Barbara. There had to be two hundred people who showed up when they arrived in Santa Barbara. Juan was one of them. Everyone cheered; several yelled out, "let's hang them."

# CHAPTER 25

Sometimes the best laid plans don't come to fruition. With the capture of Captain Suarez and his six Dragoons, the recapture of Ernesto Hernandez and the nabbing of four of General Lopez' staff, the entire case against the soldiers sent to capture Santana and St. Pierre took on a different perspective. For the five days that Tommy and his group were tracking the escapee, Joshua Black, John Wroster and Juan Sanchez looked at their case and what the jail break did to their plans.

In essence they game planned two scenarios. How would they try the various individuals involved if Tommy Sanchez didn't bring the Dragoons and Hernandez back? The second scenario would be if he did bring them back. Knowing his step father's capability, Juan thought the chances were seventy to thirty that Tommy would be successful. Juan realized they couldn't pursue a trial now as though there was just one issue. Realistically, there were now four different cases and as prosecutor, he had to petition the court to gain more time and break up the indictments.

After careful thought, a warrant was issued for the arrest of General Lopez who was charged with planning, aiding and abetting the Santa Barbara jail break. Juan knew he'd claim diplomatic immunity, but he didn't care. Even if they didn't bring him in, they'd put him on trial for the jail break and for conspiracy to invade California.

Juan sent an arrest warrant by courier to the Pinkerton Detective Agency in Los Angeles. James J. Patterson immediately went to the Consul Generale's office in downtown Los Angeles. He was unable to serve the warrant, because the General wasn't there and no one would tell Jefferson where he went.

When Jefferson reported what happened, Juan got permission from the city council to expend funds to hire the Pinkertons to find, arrest and bring back Lopez.

Juan petitioned the trial judge for a hearing on the four aspects of his cases, which was granted two days later. With his two consultants with him, plus opposing counsel, he addressed the judge. "Your honor, although the invasion of the Mexican Soldiers, the spying by Ernesto Hernandez and the jail break and subsequent capture of the perpetrators of the break are all related, my office can't do justice for the people of this state nor the defendants, by trying them all together."

"What are you suggesting Mr.. Sanchez?"

"I'm asking the court to consider four separate trials. I'd like to keep the same trial date for the Mexican Soldiers or Volunteers as they like to be called. Two months later, I want to try those Mexican Soldiers who planned and executed the jail break of Ernesto Hernandez together with the four members of General Lopez' staff. The third trial should be for General Lopez who planned the Santa Barbara jailbreak. The fourth trial will be for Ernesto Hernandez, who is accused of spying for a foreign government.

"Mr. Vargas, your thoughts?"

"I have several objections. I believe counselor's request puts too much of a hardship on Mr. Hernandez who if Mr. Sanchez has his way will be incarcerated for an undetermined amount of time while the other three trials take precedence, especially since he's in jail on a trumped up charge of spying."

"The case against the Mexican Volunteers must be tried in US Federal Court. Santa Barbara County doesn't have jurisdiction. The same analogy applies to the seven Dragoons who attempted a jail break. As far as General Lopez is concerned, he has diplomatic immunity as do the four members of his staff."

"Your honor, our contention is that Mr. Hernandez gave information to General Lopez on the whereabouts of Mr. Santana and Robert St. Pierre. With that information, General Lopez orchestrated an invasion of our state where our people were killed and an attempted kidnapping took place. Mr. Hernandez is a key element in everything that happened, starting with the invasion. There has to be a reason why seven men came from Los Angeles to break Mr. Hernandez and him alone out of our jail. I suggest that if we release Mr. Hernandez, he will be a flight risk and the people won't have an opportunity to see whether he's guilty or not or how the information he provided to the Mexican Government resulted in all the charges being brought by this county."

"The jail break is a state crime and as such should be tried by the people of California. The crimes the Volunteers are charged with are also state crimes, not federal. Our contention is that

General Lopez is the architect of the invasion by the Volunteers and the orchestrator of the jail break. He should not be granted diplomatic immunity but should be charged where the crime was committed."

"Your honor, General Lopez has diplomatic immunity and can't be tried by the State of California. So the nexus can't be proven. Therefore, I object to continued incarceration of Mr. Hernandez. In addition, since General Lopez has diplomatic immunity, he cannot be tried for either of the two charges against him."

"Mr. Vargas, can you explain to the court why seven men came from Los Angeles to break Mr. Hernandez, an American citizen and only Mr. Hernandez out of jail while many of your Mexican Countrymen were ignored and left in jail?"

"I don't have that answer at this time, your honor. I do have another objection that I would like to raise at this time' if your honor will permit it." The judge acknowledged his approval.

"The four men who are arrested along with those charged with jail breaking, have nothing to do with the jail break. They only provided food and water to the dragoons. There's no proof that they were involved in anything but an altruistic attitude toward seven men who were hungry and thirsty.

"Mr. Vargas you'll have ample opportunity to disprove the charges at trial." The judge smiled at Mr. Vargas.

"Mr. Sanchez, prepare the paperwork for the trial dates for the individuals as you suggested and I'll sign them."

Tommy and the others took a few days to recover from their tedious tracking of Suarez and the Dragoons Juan had been working non stop for a month and he and Linda decided they would take the weekend off and go to their home on Rancho del Prado. They arrived Friday night late but saw Sarah and Tommy on their way to their house. They didn't stop long but he and Tommy agreed to go fishing tomorrow afternoon around one.

Linda prepared lunch and Tommy brought wine and all the fishing gear. They toasted each other and looked forward to a good day of fishing.

Juan brought Tommy up to speed on the trials approved by the court. "What are your thoughts?" Juan asked his step-father.

"I think you've found your leverage. You should go through with the four trials and make it known that you won't discuss any deals until all the trials are over and verdicts issued. The best chance you have for a verdict in any of the trials and the greatest leverage to restrict the Mexicans from coming after the two families again is Suarez and the dragoons."

"The Feds may not get involved. I think the jail break irritated them as much as it did you. If you can get a conviction and hold Suarez and the Dragoons in jail for the term of their sentence, you'll restrict the Mexicans from taking any action against Santana and St. Pierre. You never can tell, the Mexican Government may even want to turn on General Lopez. I'll bet he's hiding from them as much as he's hiding from you."

"The trials will drive the Feds crazy, let alone the Mexicans who'll be pressuring the Feds to intercede. Keeping Hernandez incarcerated will put tremendous pressure on him. I bet he gives you everything you want on Lopez before he goes to trial." Tommy smiled.

# CHAPTER 26

After a jury of twelve men was selected, Juan gave his introductory presentation, starting his opening statement with the essence of the tenth amendment of the United States Constitution. "The powers not specifically delegated to the federal government, and not specifically prohibited by state law, belong to the states."

Intuitively he knew the jury was paying attention. Everyone had been reading the newspaper account leading up to the trial, because of all the letters to the editor. They knew what the state's position was as well as that of the federal government. Those selected for this jury knew that either way the verdict went, they would be making history.

The Mexican Defense Attorney, Henri Vargas had made three separate motions last week. Each was for a change of venue for the trials. The court denied the motions and the trials were to take place in Santa Barbara. Today Vargas decided to postpone his opening statement until later.

The initial witness called by Juan was the foreman of Mrs. Cota's Rancho, Juan Herrera. In Spanish, with an interpreter present, he told the jury how the Mexican Invasion Group had fired at will at his vaqueros, who were unarmed. Two of his men were shot and killed as the Mexicans made their way to the St. Pierre Farm. The two men killed were born in the United States; one of them was married and left a wife and two children.

Herrera told the jury that he was born in Mexico City, Mexico and had been in the United States for five years. He had a wife and two children and had applied for US Citizenship. Under cross examination by the English Speaking Mexican lawyer, he denied that his men had provoked the Mexicans into shooting at them. He scored some points for Juan when he said, "how could we provoke them? We were unarmed and they were trespassing."

Jose Santana told the jury that he and his son Fernando were outside when the Mexicans came upon them. The invaders started firing immediately; he and his son ran to the house. They were under continuous fire inside the house until three of the invaders crashed through the rear wall, grabbed their daughter, tore her dress and made off with her.

Under cross examination by Vargas, he was asked about the gold he stole from the Mexican Government when he was on Maximilian's staff. Before Jose could respond, Juan objected and produced the agreement the Mexicans signed in Albuquerque which stated that no funds were stolen from the Mexican Government.

The judge called an adjournment at noon for two hours, so the jury could have lunch. Juan knew that the Mexican's case would rest on Tommy Sanchez' testimony Vargas would show no mercy. Juan had briefed Tommy on their potential cross, but Tommy didn't seem concerned.

Sarah, her daughter and husband, Naomi, Franklin Sutter and his wife, Enrique Guitterez and the St. Pierre and Santana families lined the front row behind Juan and Tommy.

Juan led Tommy through his biographical data, his business history and his relationship with the sheriff and the two families who were invaded by the Mexicans. He asked him if he and his men fired on the fleeing Mexicans. "I ordered two rounds to make them stop and make them recognize we controlled the escape route. Two of their men were killed."

"What happened next?"

"Their commander came with a white flag and told us they had captured Maria Santana and were taking her to Mexico." I gave him an ultimatum that they either surrender or they would die trying to escape. He said he would talk it over with his men. Subsequently, he came back with the white flag and said they were going to Mexico. I told him if that was his answer I was going to shoot him now. He asked for another conference with his men, which I granted. When he returned, he said he and his men would surrender."

"Did you tell the Mexican Commander that you didn't care what happened to the hostage, Maria Santana?"

"No. I told their commander that anything that happened to the girl was on his head."

"Would you have killed all the intruders?"

"That was up to them, I was firm when I said there would be no escape. My feeling was that if we allowed them to escape with Maria, her parents would never see her again. She would be used as leverage to accomplish their objective. They wanted St. Pierre and Santana.    I Told

Captain Rodriquez that he either surrendered or he and his men would die. They could easily see there was no escape. We controlled access to the beach, we controlled the beach and their reinforcements on the boat couldn't help them. Their commander did the correct thing."

"Your witness." Juan turned Tommy over to the Mexican Defense attorney..

'So you're the son of Sitting Bull, who massacred General Custer and all his men at the Battle of the Little Big Horn?' Before Tommy could answer, Juan objected and the trial judge upheld his objection.

"Mr. Sanchez isn't it true that your wife Sarah was the former wife of Crazy Horse the Indian who led the massacre on General Custer and his men?"

Juan was out of his seat immediately and yelled "objection."

The judge upheld the objection.

Before the defense attorney could continue his cross examination of Tommy Sanchez, Juan asked for a side bar. The judge granted it and both attorneys approached the bench. "Your honor, it's obvious that the defense attorney doesn't seek to ask any pertinent questions of Mr. Sanchez to clear his clients. He more interested in embarrassing Mr. Sanchez, who committed no crime and did nothing but save lives."

"I agree. You'll confine your question to points relevant to the case. If not, I'll instruct the jury what your intent is. Do you understand me?" The judge looked directly at the defense attorney, who acknowledged that he understood.

Seeing that his hands were tied by the judge, Miguel Vargas had only one more question for Tommy. "Was the woman injured in any way while she was in the custody of the Mexican Soldiers?"

"I have no idea. Her dress was torn and parts of her body exposed. However, it's my experience that the psychological impact is difficult to measure and could last many years to come. She is a young woman, who hadn't been born when her family left Mexico and shouldn't have been kidnapped. She was a non-combatant."

When Juan rested the state's case, Mr. Vargas called Juan Rodriquez. When he was sworn in, he stated that he was the leader of the volunteers who came to California at the request of family members of the soldiers who were killed at two checkpoints by Juan Santana and Robert St. Pierre formerly of Maximilian's staff.

He testified that he didn't order his men to fire on Mrs. Cota's vaqueros. Later under encouragement by Mr. Vargas, he insisted that his men didn't fire on them. It was friendly fire from the groups supporting Santana and St. Pierre that killed them.

Under cross-examination, Rodriquez denied that he was a career soldier. Juan was able to acquire some files from Mexico that clearly stated that Rodriquez was commissioned twenty years ago, promoted to Captain ten years ago and was a career officer Juan had copies of his efficiency ratings by his commander Colonel Fidora. Juan made life unmerciful for Rodriquez until finally, the Captain utilized his rights under the Fifth Amendment. It was the only thing left for Rodriquez. His credibility was entirely destroyed.

Vargas made a motion to have the trial turned over to the Federal Government, so his country could work out a solution country to country. "If the trial attorney would just cooperate with the two governments, we could settle the issue very easily." The court took the motion under advisement and would rule before the case was sent to the jury

At the same time, one of the attorneys for the US Attorney General's Office met with Juan and came directly to the point. He threatened to send troops unless Juan immediately turned the case over to the Federal Government.

"You're wasting your time if you're threatening me. If you send troops, they may not be allowed off the boat or train. Where does that put you? This place is angry and your threats mean nothing. If you sent troops, we'll have a rebellion. Is that what you want?"

"Turn them over to us and everything goes away."

The judge denied the motion to turn the case over to the Federal Government and the case went to the jury. They deliberated for twenty-four hours and returned a verdict of guilty and recommended the death penalty for everyone. Vargas immediately filed an appeal to the California Court of Appeals. Juan had about thirty days before he tried the seven Dragoons for breaking Hernandez out of jail.

# CHAPTER 27

It seemed as though the entire federal government was interested in the case against the Mexican Soldiers who tried to kidnap Santana and St. Pierre. In Juan's perspective, no one cared about the seven dragoons nor the four staff members on General Lopez' staff. The trial for Captain Suarez, the six dragoons and the four staff members went quickly even though Mr. Vargas tried again to paint Tommy Sanchez as the villain.

Juan pointed out that Captain Suarez and the six dragoons were all on the staff of General Lopez, as were the four who were arrested with them. When he asked each of the defendants who ordered them to execute the jail break, each said he didn't know. James Jefferson was called to the stand by Juan and he summarized the Pinkerton Agency's involvement and the whereabouts of General Lopez. "What's your best guess as to the location of General Lopez?" Juan asked.

Jefferson responded clearly. "I believe he's in hiding in Mexico."

Juan knew that he didn't have any proof that the four members of General Lopez staff had anything to do with the jail break. But his instinct was that they might add something. He went after them hard and painted them as planners of the break and that they met the seven dragoons near Oxnard to see how their plan was executed. Mr. Vargas did his best but Juan was very persuasive and the four probably saw which way the jury was leaning. With the apparent defection of General Lopez, they probably wondered if their government would help them. Juan asked the jury to find all twelve defendants on trial guilty of planning and assisting in the jail break of Ernesto Hernandez.

The day before the judge gave instructions to the jury, the four members of General Lopez staff sent a message to Juan asking him if he'd be interested if they gave evidence against their fellow perpetrators, in return for leniency. They pooled their money and hired a local attorney; Juan agreed to meet with them.

Three jailers brought the four Mexicans and Senor Vegas, their attorney to Juan's office in the courthouse. Mr. Vegas asked Juan if he would grant leniency if they turned state's evidence. "I would be very interested if what they tell me helps my case against the seven dragoons and General Lopez."

One of the four, who was more articulate, told Juan they were involved in the planning, the logistics and the execution of the jail break. "General Lopez directed every aspect of the case including the earlier operation against the two French families. I know he was in direct contact with President Diaz. He told me that he had to succeed because he told the President, that he could get the job done."

"Okay here's what I want from you. You'll testify in court against the seven dragoons and General Lopez.. In addition, you'll testify in the trial against Ernesto Hernandez and General Lopez about the planning and execution of the Invasion into California to kidnap Santana and St. Pierre. I want an acknowledgement that you understand and accept the terms."

Their attorney Senor Vegas polled each of the staff officers individually and each accepted the terms.

The jury was brought back into court and testimony taken from all four staff members. Juan noticed the glares from the seven dragoons when they heard the four testify against them and

General Lopez. The dragoons knew at that moment that no one would come to rescue them. They were going to be found guilty.

Mr. Vegas had one more request for Juan. "I'm filing a petition with your state department requesting asylum for the four staff members. I would hope that you would endorse that request Mr. Sanchez. It may save their lives.

"I'll seriously consider your request."

The jury found all seven dragoons guilty of breaking Ernesto Hernandez out of jail. General Lopez was found guilty of ordering and directing the break. The four staff members were found guilty but the jury recommended that their sentences be suspended per Juan Sanchez' request with the concurrence of the judge.. The net result was the jury recommended a maximum sentence under the law for the seven dragoons and General Lopez.. The judge set the sentencing hearing for one week after the jury's verdict. During that hearing, he sentenced all the dragoons and General Lopez to a term of fifteen years each.

Vargas filed his appeal to the California Court of Appeals. There was no outrage from the Mexican Government. In fact Mr. Vargas, who was representing the seven, dragoons, rarely went to the jail to talk to them. It seemed to Juan that the dragoons and even General Lopez were expendable.

The other major surprise that Juan experienced during the trials was a visit from a local attorney by the name of Jose Cota. His practice was in Santa Barbara and he mainly handled routine cases involving Mexicans new to the area. He rarely appeared in court, but now he had a signed statement from Ernesto Hernandez naming him as his counsel of record.

"Are you telling me that Mr. Vargas has been removed from Mr. Hernandez case, which is to go to trial next month?" Juan asked Cota.

Cota produced the notification to the court that Vargas had been removed and he was Hernandez counsel. "I'm here today to discuss an alternative to going to court if that is possible?"

"What do you have in mind?"

"Mr. Hernandez will plead guilty to passing information to General Lopez that was a prelude to the invasion by the Mexican Soldiers."

"And what does Mr. Hernandez want for this information?"

"We want a sentence that involves no jail time and no fine. If he turns against General Lopez and the Mexican Government, he must be allowed to stay in the United States. If not, his life wouldn't be worth much in his native country.. How about a five year suspended sentence. If he poses no problem during the five years, he can go on with his life and any record of a sentence would be expunged. He's a gullible individual who was victimized by General Lopez."

"I'll want a complete confession including how all this went down. If I'm satisfied with what he says, I'll amend the charges and recommend to the court a suspended sentence of five years with no jail time."

Cota made a motion to the court that Hernandez would plead guilty and provide information relative to the invasion of California by Mexican Soldiers. Three days later, court was convened and Ernesto Hernandez took the stand, without a jury. Juan and his two consultants were present as was Mr. Cota, Ernesto's attorney. When court was called into session, Hernandez was worn in and Juan led him through a series of questions about the invasion.

Hernandez testified that he grew up in Mexico and was acquainted with Jose Lopez, who later would become Consul Generale in Los Angeles. Hernandez was a successful merchant and he and his family came to America and bought a small ranch in the Santa Ynez Valley about four years ago. It was Lopez who sought him out and introduced him to many of the influential Mexicans living in America. "There wasn't a month that went by during our four years in the United States when we weren't invited to some party at a beautiful home or rancho. In retrospect, my family and I were being recruited."

"When did General Lopez ask you about the St, Pierre's and the Santana's?"

"About three years ago we were at a party at one of the large ranches in the Los Angeles area. Elite Mexicans were there as well as General Lopez and the Attorney General of Mexico. Someone starting discussing what happened several years ago at two checkpoints in northern Mexico. Ten border guards were shot and left for dead by two families loyal to Maximilian. There were two unsuccessful attempts to capture and bring them back for trial in Mexico."

"Why was that significant?"

"One of the guests at the party said they were not only murderers but thieves as well. They stole gold out of the Mexican treasury before they escaped."

"How did you know they were in California?"

Hernandez leaned back and responded. "Someone said they'd been spotted in the small town of Los Alamos which was north of Santa Barbara. I don't know who said it initially, but the Mexican Attorney General asked everyone present to be on the lookout for them. If they were spotted, the Attorney General asked that he or General Lopez be informed."

"Didn't you feel disloyal to your adopted country when you became involved?"

"From what everyone was saying at the party, these people were cold-blooded killers. I felt they needed to be brought to justice."

"So it was you that spotted them and reported their exact location to General Lopez? Tell us about that."

"I went to Mrs. Cota's ranch in Los Alamos to find a breeding mare for my stallion. While I was there, one of her vaqueros indicated that they had new neighbors. I wasn't seeking them out. I was just involved in a conversation with someone in my native tongue and they told me about the two French Families. I reported what I found out to General Lopez the next time we met. I had nothing else to do with the Mexican invasion. That's all I know.

The Mexican invaders say that they are volunteers, who are seeking justice for the relatives of the border guards who were supposedly killed by Robert St. Pierre and Jose Santana. Are the Mexican Invaders soldiers in the Mexican Army or are they volunteers?"

"General Lopez told me personally that they were Mexican Soldiers."

"You honor, I would like to have the rest of the day to make a decision whether I want to amend the charges against Ernesto Hernandez," Juan said.

# CHAPTER 28

The first thing that Juan did when he returned to the office was to reread his response to the appeal by the Mexican Soldiers of their guilty verdict. He spent the next two hours with his two consultant attorneys and directed Black to write a supplement to his response to the appeal to include the Hernandez testimony. Black finished it the next day and submitted it to the court of appeals who hadn't ruled on the appeal yet.

Juan hoped that the new testimony indicating that the Mexicans were soldiers and not volunteers would be significant. The second aspect of the new evidence that seemed more important to Juan was the planning of the invasion into the sovereign state of California at the direction of the President of Mexico. Furthermore, it was implemented at the direction of his representative while serving in his official capacity as Consul Generale in California.

Juan had a choice to make. Did he want to pursue General Lopez as the planner of the jail break? The answer by he and his two consultants was yes. Ernesto Hernandez would be his key witness. He should be able to obtain a conviction, especially since General Lopez was nowhere to be found.

When the trial started, Vargas was still the attorney of record for General Lopez and he made a motion that the trial was unnecessary. "The jury has given Hernandez a five year suspended sentence and General Lopez is nowhere to be found. "What's the point in wasting everyone's time?" He asked the judge.

Juan responded. General Lopez is being charged with planning and directing the jail break to free Ernesto Hernandez. To date the charges haven't been before the jury. We intend to call Ernesto Hernandez and the four men on General Lopez staff who participated in the planning and logistics of the break."

"Motion denied, call your first witness Mr. Sanchez."

"The state calls Ernesto Hernandez." Juan walked Hernandez through the lead up to the jail break and what happened afterward. Hernandez testified that he was surprised when the dragoons came to the jail. He asked his rescuers why they did it. Three of them including Captain Suarez said that General Lopez wanted to reward him for his silence. It was Lopez who ordered the operation.

Each of the four staffers for General Lopez told the same story. General Lopez had them develop a plan to rescue Ernesto Hernandez in the Santa Barbara jail. At least two of them were present when they received a communiqué from President Diaz to rescue Hernandez. Each of the two saw the communication. Vargas continually objected to all the testimony but in the end, Juan kept his patience and was able to have all the testimony he needed in the record.

The jury retired after receiving the judge's instructions and took three hours to find General Lopez guilty of directing a jailbreak at the Santa Barbara jail. Mr. Vargas immediately filed an appeal to the California Court of Appeals.

Juan decided to go to Rancho Del Prado with his wife Linda. She was about seven months along in her pregnancy and he was tired. He left Mr. Black to man his office in case any or all of the appeals were decided. He was at his home for two days before he contacted his stepfather and mother. The four had dinner in the kitchen and after a couple of glasses of wine, Juan fell asleep. He and Linda stayed in the guest room rather than travel at night back to their new home.

At breakfast the next morning, Juan was back to his old self and openly discussed the progress of the three cases. "We haven't heard anything from the Appeals Court on the three cases. They don't work as fast as us and they have a lot to think about. Mr. Wroster has considerable background in appellate work and he's been in Sacramento since the first case was appealed. I talked to him three days ago and he promised to let me know the instant they decide. He knows they have the three cases and should take them in order, but I can't count on that happening."

"What's your best guess on the appeals?" Tommy asked.

"To be honest, I don't know. One of the US State Department Attorneys is in Sacramento using all his influence and the word from his office is that he doesn't know what they'll do. Our government has caved in before in New Mexico. Probably some of those who made the decision to give the soldiers back are still there. The information that the four staffers and Hernandez gave implicating President Diaz could be the decider."

"I really don't know when this will end. If the appeals court decides in our favor, Vargas can appeal to the California Supreme Court and then on to the US Supreme Court."

# CHAPTER 29

Two months after the three trials ended Linda Sanchez gave birth to a seven-pound baby boy. The couple immediately named him Thomas Sitting Bull Sanchez. Tommy and Sarah were present at the hospital when the event took place. When informed that their grandson would be named after Tommy, Sarah cried and Tommy took a long walk. A week later the three members of the Juan Sanchez family came home to Rancho Del Prado, but Sarah insisted they stay in their guest room. She would be a doting grandmother.

Over the next four months, the three cases went through the appeal process. The case against General Lopez was refused to be heard by the California Supreme Court after the state's appeal court ruled in favor of Santa Barbara County. Vargas filed an appeal to The US Supreme Court. The same thing happened to the case against the seven dragoons. Neither of these cases was heard by the California Supreme Court or Appeals Court.

Vargas did everything he could to secure the release of all the defendants in the three cases, but to date, the County of Santa Barbara stood strong and all those convicted, were still in jail. Unless politics raised its head, the seven dragoons were going to serve fifteen years in the Santa Barbara County jail. All seven felt they were forgotten

The California Supreme Court overturned the case against the soldiers who invaded California to kidnap St. Pierre and Santana. They ruled that the county of Santa Barbara didn't have jurisdiction on the case. Juan immediately filed an appeal to the US Court of Appeals, who refused to hear the case. Subsequently, Juan filed an appeal to the US Supreme Court. One month later four of the justices agreed to hear his appeal. The court refused to hear Mr. Vargas two appeals. Therefore, the cases against the Dragoons and General Lopez were finalized.

When Juan heard the news, he was in his office in Santa Ynez. He came home immediately to tell his wife, mother and stepfather. "I was asked by the County Board of Supervisors to present the county's argument to the Supreme Court. I'm just a small-town attorney. There are others more qualified than I that should present our case."

"You've handled all three cases with two consultants. Not only that but you've withstood the might of the US Department of State. You can handle it. Everyone in this room knows you can handle this and I believe so do you. Make us proud. You have the right stuff." Tommy hugged his step-son.

Juan, his step-father and mother arrived in the nation's capitol a week before the date of his presentation before the Supreme Court. Linda stayed home with the new baby. Tommy had never been here before but Sarah had come years earlier with her first husband, Crazy Horse. While Juan was preparing his argument, his parents enjoyed the nightlife and took a carriage to see all the monuments.

Finally, the court was in session and oral arguments were scheduled. The finest attorneys in Washington DC were hired by the Mexican Government to handle their case The State Department was in attendance.

Juan's oral argument was straightforward. They were invaded, people were killed and they captured the guilty people involved. They must be punished. The people of Santa Barbara County are seeking the death penalty.

"Doesn't the disposition of this case belong to the US State Department? The chief justice asked.

"Your honor, the facts state that fifteen volunteers from the country of Mexico came into our county with the express purpose of kidnapping two individuals. They were unsuccessful, but in the course of their deed, they kidnapped an American Citizen, Maria Santana with the express purpose of using her as a hostage to complete their objective. That makes this a state case. There are signed affidavits by all the Mexicans that participated in this raid that they were strictly volunteers, not Mexican soldiers."

"But you know that's a sham. All the records show that they were sworn into the Mexican Military."

"Your honor, my job is to follow the facts wherever they may lead. Each of those men presented to the court affidavits that swore they weren't Mexican Soldiers."

When the Mexican lead attorney finished his rebuttal, Justice Stevens asked him. "Didn't the State Department take over the case in New Mexico, after the Mexican Government sent soldiers to kidnap St.Pierre and Santana?"

"Yes your honor. We then negotiated with the Mexican Government and a reasonable solution was reached that benefitted both countries."

"Will you tell the court what the reasonable conditions were?"

"Your honor, I was not a party to those negotiations."

"You mean you're not prepared to discuss this issue thoroughly?"

"Your honor, I have the agreement before me and it's part of the package submitted by the State Department."

"Didn't the Mexican Government promise never to invade our country again to kidnap the two former Maximilian's aides?'

"Yes your honor."

The session was over in ninety minutes and Juan, his two consultants, Tommy and Sarah took the train back to California. Juan felt good about his presentation and so was his family.

Two months later the same Mexican Government attorney who contested Juan's appeal to the Supreme Court came to Santa Barbara California along with representatives form the California Governor's Office and US State Department and two high level representatives from the Mexican Government. They asked to meet with Juan and his consultants

"I'd rather not meet until we hear from the Supreme Court."

"We're coming at the express recommendation of the Chief Justice of the US Supreme Court. He wants us to meet one more time to see if we can come to a reasonable conclusion." John Jacobs said.

"If that's true, then the Chief Justice would've sent me official word."

"He did. I'm the courier of that communiqué."

Juan read the letter and handed it to Black and Wroster to read. He turned to the Mexican Government Attorney. "Let's set a meeting for one PM tomorrow in my office in the Courthouse."

Juan turned to Black and Wroster. "What do you think of this?"

"The Supreme Court is throwing us a bone. They want you to negotiate a reasonable settlement, but they're not restricting our parameters." Black responded

"Let's put them off for three days. We need somebody from the Board of Supervisors in on this. They are our client. Joshua, would you tell The Mexicans we need a few days. What do you say?' Juan said

Black was excited about the turn of events. "The opposition is staying at the Arlington. I think two days from now is enough.. We know what we want, so let's see how hard they want to negotiate. I'll tell them."

That afternoon, Juan met with the Chairman of the Board of Supervisors, William Watson, and told him what was going on. "Whoever you pick, it should be someone who's smart enough to stay out of the way and let us negotiate."

"It's going to be me and yes, I'll let you handle the negotiation. You've done great so far and I believe you and your consultants can pull it off. I'll meet with the other supervisors and County Counsel to see what they say. I'll be waiting for your call."

The three worked through the next night, slept in the jail until one in the afternoon and reconvened. By the time of their meeting with the other side they felt comfortable with their position.

When the time came everyone involved sat around a large table in the conference room in the Santa Barbara Courthouse. Frank Sturges, an Under-Secretary within the US State Department stood up and said that they'd gotten together and came up with a position they could live with and he handed out copies of their position to Juan, his consultants and the Chairman of the Board of Supervisors. He sat down and Juan and his group read the proposal.

The county of Santa Barbara would release all the Volunteers, the Dragoons and Mr. Hernandez immediately upon signing an agreement with all the parties present.

All charges against these individuals would be dropped and any record of their trials would be expunged.

The Mexican Government would promise not to make any further attempt to bring Robert St, Pierre and Jose Santana to Justice.

The Mexican Government will pay reparations to the St. Pierre's and Santana's the sum of Ten Thousand dollars for the inconvenience and five hundred each to the two Vaqueros who worked for Mrs. Cota and were killed during the incursion

The four read the short document, huddled for a few minutes before Juan addressed everyone. "We've read the document and here's our response." Juan tore his copy of the document in half and then quarters and dropped it on the table.

The silence that followed was almost deafening. Finally, Sturges mumbled. "You can't be serious. That was a good offer."

Nobody said anything for a least two minutes before Juan rose again. "Gentlemen, this is what a good proposal looks like." He handed out a twenty-page document to all members of the opposition. "Please come back here tomorrow at one PM and be prepared to agree to negotiate the terms of this proposal. Good day, gentlemen."

The major items within Juan's proposal were:

1. The Volunteers would be released but if any of them returned to the United States or their territory, they'd be arrested and the sentence given by the court would be enforced.

2. The seven Dragoons would serve out their sentence given by the court.

3. General Lopez" sentence will be enforced.

4. The two former aides to Maximilian would be paid Twenty-Five Thousand Dollars each.

5. The families of two dead Vaqueros who worked for Mrs. Cota will receive One thousand dollars each.

6. Santa Barbara County will be paid a total of Fifty Thousand Dollars for the damages done by the Dragoons.

7. Hernandez' suspended sentence will remain as is.

Sturges was red in the face when he responded. "You can't be serious. This offer is a non-starter. The Mexicans won't agree to any of this."

"Why don't we hear from them? They're sitting next to you."

Pedro Lopez, the senior Mexican Government Representative said in Spanish that anything agreed to must be approved by President Diaz.

"Gentlemen, the Mexican Government has invaded our country three times to kidnap the two former aides. We don't want this to happen again. If the Mexicans decide they're going to come a fourth time, we want them to know it's going to be costly. Mr. Lopez, I suggest you get some parameters from President Diaz, because this is our proposal and we intend to stand behind it."

Sturges wasn't finished. "You can't get away with this form of blackmail."

Juan smiled. "Perhaps you could spend more of your time trying to reach an agreement rather than be an adversary. Perhaps your team might be better served with a new spokesman. I hope to hear from you gentlemen within a week."

"Will you show some good faith by releasing the volunteers pending the resolution of an agreement? Sturges asked.

"No"

# CHAPTER 30

It took a month before the Mexicans reported back to the group. Their position was that all Mexican Nationals will be released. General Lopez is to be exonerated and the two Maximilian Aides will return the gold they took when they left Mexico.

Juan met with his group and it was unanimous. They would stay with their proposal. The Supreme Court didn't seem to be putting a timeline on an agreement. "I say we stay with what we want and force the Mexicans to make concessions before we do."

Juan took the weekend off, His wife and child traveled with him to Rancho Del Prado, On Saturday he went fishing with his step-father and brought him up to speed.

"It seems to me that the Mexican Government has made some concessions. But they haven't dropped the gold. I'm just wondering out loud if they might be right." Tommy said.

"Robert and Jose have sworn to both of us that they didn't take any gold."

"I know. I know. But what if both sides are correct? Is that possible?
"What do you mean?"

"I think you and I should visit Jose and Robert. We've worked hard to keep them safe. They owe us some answers to our questions."

'When do you want to do that?"

"I'll call Franklin and see if he can set up a meeting on Monday. Would that work for you?"

"I could stay another couple of days if it would help."

Tommy told Franklin they wanted to talk to Robert and Jose to bring them up to date on the negotiations with the Mexicans and our State Department. A few hours later, Franklin responded that anytime Monday Morning would be okay.

Juan and Tommy took the train first thing Monday Morning and were picked up by Franklin at the station. He took them both to the farm where Jose met them. "Robert and I are available now if you want to talk to us."

Tommy shook both their hands. "We'd like to talk to both you and your wives if that's possible."

"Sure, no problem. Let's go in the house and we'll ask the wives to join us."

After they had coffee, the six sat down around the kitchen table. Juan summarized what his position was and what the Mexicans countered with, "The sticking issue from my viewpoint is the gold they say was taken from their treasury."

"Juan we've told you over and over again we didn't steal the gold. Neither I nor Robert had anything to do with taking it. Why can't they believe us." Jose was irritated.

"Jose, I believe you and Robert and I believe the Mexicans think they are correct. I think both sides are telling the truth. However, I believe the gold was taken into the United States and its here in California." Tommy said.

"Then you're saying Jose and I lied and we stole the gold."

"On the contrary, I believe you. So if it's here, how did it get here?  I don't know exactly, but is it possible that it was in your wagons when you left Mexico." Tommy said.

Jose was furious and got out of his chair and pointed at Tommy. "If you call us a liar again, I'm going to challenge you. I don't care about your reputation. You can't come into our house and insult us."

It was as though it was a whisper that no one heard. "There will be no challenge. He's correct." Angelica said.

As soon as she made the statement another voice said "No, Angelica."

"Sophia, it has to come out. Too many people have been hurt; some have died and it's not going away"

Jose looked at his wife. "What are you saying?"

Tommy put his hand on Jose's arm. "Let her tell us what happened."

Everyone turned to face Angelica. "Most of the gold they say is missing was taken by

Carlotta. She didn't think Max was going to last and she wanted to be sure they'd be well taken care of when they went back to Europe. Max had no place to go after Franz Josef made him relinquish his title. When Carlotta was ready to leave, she called Sophia and me into her chambers. She told us about the gold that she'd taken from the treasury. She had access because she was regent when Max was out of the city."

"I don't know how much she took back to Europe but it was a lot. She reflected that Max wasn't going to last much longer and for the four of us to get out of Mexico. She put aside about fifty thousand dollars for us and told us to hide it in our furniture and leave Mexico immediately."

"We were introduced to a furniture maker by Carlotta and he was able to fashion extra shelving in our dining room furniture that could hide the gold bars. It took him two months to finish the job. He thought we were going to hide our jewels and money there in case we were stopped by robbers while trying to leave. We kept the gold hidden there until we arrived in San Francisco. We met a gold merchant and sold the gold the afternoon we said we were going shopping. We then opened up a savings account and placed the funds in the account under Sophia's name and mine. Once you men said we didn't have the gold, what were we to say?" Angelica broke down and cried.

"Why didn't you tell us about it?"

With all the trouble, we were afraid of what you would say."

"You told our children we didn't steal the gold. How could you do that?' Jose was furious.

Tommy knew he had to settle everyone down. "The Mexicans want their gold back, but they haven't objected to Juan's demand that they give each of the families twenty-five thousand dollars. Why not give the gold back that you're afraid to use for the twenty-five thousand each of you can use without any guilt?"

"But they'll still come after us and use the gold as an incentive," Sophia said.

"No matter what we agree to, all of us feel that we're on solid ground if we keep the Dragoons in jail for fifteen years. That should hold the Mexicans in check. The big question is, can we retrieve the gold that was taken? We can always use the story that your four Mexican bodyguards stole the gold. Who's to say they didn't? Juan smiled.

"Can we talk this over just between ourselves? We don't mean to be a stumbling block for you, but we need to talk this over privately and with our children." Jose said.

"What do you think, they'll do.?" Juan asked Tommy on the way back to Santa Ynez.

"I think they'll give the gold back. It's really out in the open and it's a win-win for them with very little fallout."

# CHAPTER 31

Jose and Robert with their wives went to San Francisco to see if they could retrieve the same gold bars that their wives sold to a gold merchant. It wasn't easy and it cost them two thousand dollars from their savings but they were able to get the gold bars back.

To say that their marriages were under stress was an understatement. Robert's two sons yelled at their mother and wouldn't speak to her for nearly a month. In fact, the two young men left home for a week which caused further pain. But there was too much love in both families to have their anger last.

The negotiations stalled for a month. Finally, the Mexican and US State Department Representatives called Juan and asked for another meeting. It was as though General Lopez and his Dragoons would be fed to the lions. They negotiated hard on the fifty thousand dollars to be paid to the two families, but eventually, everyone agreed to forty thousand to be paid to the two families and the other ten thousand to be given to the ten families of the men who were killed by Robert, Jose and their bodyguards at the checkpoints.

The Mexican Government agreed not to do any harm to Robert or Jose. The gold was transferred within ten days of the signing of the agreement between all parties and approved by the US Supreme Court.

The Dragoons wanted to talk to Juan but he declined. They hired another attorney and petitioned the court for a new trial. They were willing to turn against their government for a reduced sentence. The court refused to hear their petition.

Robert and Jose sold their farm and moved out of the area. They didn't say goodbye to Tommy, Juan, or any of their friends. Rene and Armand St. Pierre married the two Wellington Sisters, Susanne and Margaret, and moved onto the Wellington Ranch. Their father welcomed them. They were hard-working men and would be good husbands to his daughters.

Carlos and his wife came to visit and the two couples became closer. They didn't discuss the Mexican Invasion and its aftermath.